Lori scanned the sky. The sun's descent was no longer visible and the dark hues of evening were beginning to take over.

"It's gone," she said softly.

"No, it's not," Ian said. "Just because a few clouds got in the way doesn't mean it's gone forever. If you use your imagination, you can light up the sky."

"And if my imagination isn't that good?"

"I'll help you. See, right there—that streak of gold trying to break through? Then the red? Now the orange?" He caught her chin with one hand and turned her face upward. The rest of his words were lost in the gentle pressure of his lips against hers.

Dear Readers,

We at Silhouette would like to thank all our readers for your many enthusiastic letters. In direct response to your encouragement, we are now publishing *four* FIRST LOVEs every month.

As always FIRST LOVEs are written especially for and about you—your hopes, your dreams, your ambitions.

Please continue to share your suggestions and comments with us; they play an important part in our pleasing you.

I invite you to write to us at the address below:

Nancy Jackson
Senior Editor
Silhouette Books
P.O. Box 769
New York, N.Y. 10019

ADVICE AND CONSENT
Bea Alexander

First Love from Silhouette

Published by Silhouette Books New York
America's Publisher of Contemporary Romance

Other First Loves by Bea Alexander

Someone Like Jeremy Vaughn

SILHOUETTE BOOKS, a Division of Simon & Schuster, Inc.
1230 Avenue of the Americas, New York, N.Y. 10020

ISBN: 0-671-53369-X

First Silhouette Books printing November, 1983

10 9 8 7 6 5 4 3 2 1

America's Publisher of Contemporary Romance

Printed in the U.S.A.

ADVICE
AND CONSENT

1

The table was already crowded and Lori didn't think some of the girls were too thrilled about moving their things to make room for her. She wouldn't even have attempted to join that particular table if Janis Jamison hadn't been so insistent.

"This is Lori Kennedy," Janis said as a place was finally cleared. "She's just transferred from Weston and I've already gotten her signed up for the decorating committee. I took one look at this kid's work in art class yesterday and I knew we just had to make use of her talents."

Most of the girls smiled and nodded, but it was obvious they weren't that interested in what Janis was saying. Lori got the distinct impression that she had arrived right in the middle of an extremely important discussion.

"She's going to absolutely transform that barn of

a gym for the next dance," Janis continued. "She's got an incredible sense of color."

Lori adjusted her tray and wondered how Janis had come to such a conclusion after seeing only one example of her work. She had been somewhat embarrassed yesterday by the girl's effusiveness in front of the other students but also somewhat grateful. She hadn't expected to find such an instant friend and ally on her first day at Lincoln High.

"And we all know how important this dance is going to be," Janis said, nodding toward a slender, redheaded girl at the far end of the table.

The girl looked as if she was about to blush.

"It may not be important at all," said the blond next to her, "if we don't solve her problem."

"We should all have such problems!" sighed a round-faced brunette next to Lori.

Another of the girls laughed and suddenly they were all talking at once. Lori reached for her fork and inspected the cafeteria food before her. It didn't look that appetizing and yet she felt extremely hungry. She took a bite of the pale gray meat and was surprised to discover how good it tasted.

Names and relationships that meant nothing to her were being discussed around the table. Lori concentrated on the food on her tray. The cafeteria at Weston had never served meals as good as this. Or maybe it was just that she was starving after what had seemed an endless gym class.

"And he *would* have to be so cute!" one of the girls exclaimed in a high-pitched voice that immediately provoked an outburst of laughter from all the others.

Lori looked up from her food and tried to smile. Some of the girls were casting glances at the cafeteria line and Lori turned her head in the same direction. She caught a glimpse of someone in a letter sweater, but he was instantly blocked from sight by a long row of metal tray holders. She got an impression of broad shoulders and a heftiness she associated with football players.

She went back to her food, hoping what was left on her plate was going to be enough to satisfy her sudden ravenous appetite.

"Well, what are you going to say?" one of the girls asked the redhead. "He's going to walk by any minute now."

"I'm not going to say anything. It's up to him."

Disagreement instantly broke out among the girls at the table.

Lori ate the last forkful of food on her plate and knew that she was going to need more if she was expected to last through her chemistry lab that afternoon. She at least had to get an apple from the vending machine.

"Just say *something* to him," Janis urged the redhead. "You've got to grab the moments when they come, and this is going to be a crucial one."

"She's got weeks before the dance!"

"Weeks in which to be miserable!"

The entire conversation was starting to sound awfully silly to Lori. All this agony and plotting over a boy who probably wasn't at all interested in the girl in question. Lori pushed her chair back from the table and got up, suddenly glad to get away from her lunchmates for a few minutes. Maybe by the time she got back they would have moved on to other topics.

The apple vending machine was to the right of the cafeteria line. Lori hesitated as she reached it, wondering perhaps if instead she should get a piece of pie. The apple would be healthier, but the pie more filling, and at the moment her stomach felt amazingly empty.

She turned toward the entrance to the line, her movement so abrupt that she bumped into the person who had just paid at the cash register.

"Excuse me," she apologized, looking down at the tray she had jostled.

"It's okay," the boy said. "Nothing's spilled."

It took her a moment to realize that he was the one the other girls had been talking about, the guy in the letter sweater with whom the redhead wanted to go to the dance. Lori glanced at his face. Yes, she supposed he was cute, but her eyes didn't linger on him long.

Something else had drawn them away, something she wasn't even consciously aware of until her eyes had refocused. Coming down the line was a tall boy in a yellow sweater. His arms and legs were long, almost gangly, and his face was surrounded by curly blond hair that belied the serious set of his lips.

Lori blinked her eyes and then blinked them again.

It couldn't be.

The boy in the letter sweater cleared his throat. "You mind if I get by?" he asked lightly.

"Oh," Lori said with embarrassment, still unable to take her eyes from the tall boy in the line. She began moving to her left and then stopped.

The boy with the broad shoulders laughed. "I still can't get by you," he said.

Lori moved a few more inches.

"I want to go the other way," he said with another laugh.

Lori frowned, her eyes still on the cafeteria line. "The table's down there," she said.

"Huh?"

"The table with that girl."

"What girl?"

"That red-haired girl," Lori said, gesturing vaguely with her arm. "The one who wants to go to the dance with you."

"What!"

Lori let her eyes leave the cafeteria line for an instant. Had she really said that last sentence aloud?

She must have done so, because the face on the boy before her changed to astonishment.

"I'm sorry," she said. "I shouldn't have—"

"You mean Laura Cooper?" he interrupted. "She really wants to go to the dance with me? Are you telling me the truth or what?"

Lori smiled guiltily. "I . . . well . . ."

"Well, yes or no?" he said, the crockery on his tray starting to jiggle because of his excitement.

"Well"—Lori felt herself gulping—"well . . . yes. But don't—"

She never got to finish her sentence. The boy was pushing past her with such eagerness that Lori thought she was going to lose her balance. She shot a glance toward the table where the other girls sat. They looked amazed to see the boy rapidly approaching.

Lori looked back toward the cafeteria line, wondering if she was going to be an outcast at Lincoln High once the girls discovered what she had just done. But she didn't have time to ponder the matter. The tall boy with the curly blond hair was at the cash register paying for his lunch.

Should she call out his name and risk making a complete fool of herself? It had to be him, and yet . . .

The boy was turning, his face still set in a serious expression. His deep blue eyes looked up from the tray in his arms and then suddenly his entire body seemed to stop in midmotion as he spotted her.

Neither said a word.

They stared at each other for a few seconds; then the smile that Lori remembered from years before shyly came to his lips and his entire face brightened. He shook his head in astonishment, setting his blond curls bouncing as he came toward her.

"It's really you, isn't it," he said finally as he stood before her. The shyness of his smile managed to color his words slightly.

"Yes, it's me, all right," she laughed.

"I suppose I should be saying that you haven't changed a bit," he said.

Lori laughed again. "Since you recognized me so easily, maybe I haven't."

"Your hair is shorter."

"Yours is longer."

"All that baby fat has totally gone."

"The same can be said for you."

It was his turn to laugh. "I never had any baby fat to begin with," he said, looking down the length of his body. "Maybe you should have sent me some of yours before you gave it away."

She made a slight face at him, but it only seemed to increase his smile.

"So, what are you doing here?" he asked finally. "Visiting friends?"

"I go to school here," Lori said.

"You're kidding! Since when?"

"Since yesterday. What about you?"

"Since two weeks ago." He paused and then whistled softly. "This is really strange. Maybe old friendships don't have to die away."

"I wanted to write," she said.

"I did, too."

"You're the one who owes me a letter."

"Doesn't that postcard count?"

"What postcard?"

"The one from Yosemite."

"That was over two years ago!"

He let out a sigh. "Well, what does it matter? We're here and we've found each other again. We can start where we left off."

"Except that this is high school and that was arts and crafts camp," Lori said. "A bit of a difference, wouldn't you say?"

"But we're still the same, aren't we?"

"We were kids five years ago."

"Oh, I'm still a kid."

Lori's eyes traveled the length of him, only to discover that his eyes were taking in the changes in her body, too. They both laughed at the same time.

A bell sounded in the hallway. Lori glanced at the clock on the side wall. There would be no time for either an apple or a piece of pie.

"I have to be going," she said.

There was disappointment in his eyes. "But we have so much to catch up on," he said. "I haven't even found out how your painting is going."

"You haven't told me about how yours is going, either," she countered.

"Where can we meet? Out front after the last bell?"

Lori nodded, but then her smile faded. "No—I forgot. I have to attend a meeting after school."

"A meeting?"

"The decorating committee for the next dance. One of the girls here thinks I have great potential in that field," she said wryly.

"Don't hide your talent under a bushel basket." He laughed.

"How come you didn't get corralled into helping out?"

"Ssh! No one here knows yet about my talents. I've avoided art class like the plague."

Lori frowned. "I don't get it."

The blue in his eyes clouded over. "Maybe it's time to put away childish things."

"Childish things!"

He ignored her remark. "I'll catch up with you tomorrow, then," he said. "Okay?"

"Okay, Ian." She was surprised at how good it felt to say his name again after all those years. The bell sounded once again. "Oh, great! I'm going to have to rush like mad now if I want to get to my chem lab on time."

"Well then, do it!" Ian laughed.

"I am! I am!" she yelled, pushing by him to get to the door. "I'll see you tomorrow."

"Yes—'til tomorrow!"

She carried his laughter with her all the way down the corridor. It had deepened considerably since she had last heard it.

"Get over here!" Janis ordered as Lori entered the art room.

Lori cringed inside as she approached her new friend. Now she was going to get it for her stupidity at lunchtime. Janis had probably been appointed by the other girls to banish her from female society at Lincoln High.

"What did you say to him?" Janis asked, drawing Lori down to one of the corner tables.

"What do you mean?" Lori had decided to act dumb for awhile until she found out how much trouble she was really in.

"Barry Jensen. What exactly did you say to him?"

"Who's Barry Jensen?"

"The football player that Laura Cooper—"

"You mean that redheaded girl?"

"Yes, that redheaded girl," Janis said with impatience. "What did you say to make it all happen?"

"To make what all happen?"

Janis stood back a few feet and gave Lori a critical look. "How come you're acting so funny? Don't you want to share your expertise with the rest of us?"

"Expertise?"

Janis brought her hand up to her short brown hair and ran her fingers through it. "Okay, suit yourself," she said finally. "But whatever it was . . . oh, Lori, please let me in on it! I'm just dying to know how you arranged it."

"Arranged what?"

"Barry's taking Laura to the dance! He asked her right in front of all of us! I mean, I thought I would die! It was so incredible! The school's been buzzing ever since."

Lori felt a sigh of relief escape. Thank goodness she wasn't going to be an outcast at Lincoln High!

"Listen," Janis said, moving in closer as other students began to fill up the room for the meeting. "Do you think you could do anything about John Kane?"

"Who's John Kane?" Lori asked, sinking down onto the top of the table.

"He sits two desks in front of you in homeroom. You know, that guy with short black hair who's not exactly skinny but who might have a good build if he did a few more push-ups."

Lori didn't know who Janis was talking about.

"Well, anyway, I was just wondering if perhaps I should be doing something different to attract his attention. I wonder if maybe you had some—"

"Hi, Lori!" The round-cheeked brunette from

the lunch table practically pushed Janis out of the way as she drew up a chair. "My name's Jennifer Logan, and I was just wondering what exactly you said to Barry Jensen that made him . . ."

Jennifer didn't get much further in her query before the next girl approached.

2

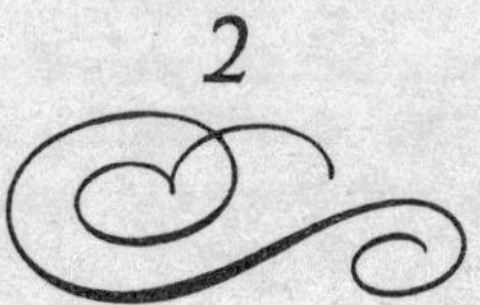

"Lori, I'm happy that you've made all these new friends so quickly," Mrs. Kennedy said as she put two slices of bread into the toaster. "And I understand about teenage girls and the telephone. But do you really think it's necessary for them to start calling at six in the morning?"

"I'm sorry about that," said Lori. She took a sip of her orange juice before glancing down at the photos on her lap. "I didn't realize they would even be calling last night. I haven't given out my number at all yet."

"Well, they must have gotten it from the phone company."

"Maybe we should get it changed," said Lori's ten-year old sister, Amanda, pulling her bowl of cornflakes dangerously close to the edge of the table. "We aren't ever going to get any sleep around here if we don't."

"I'll try to put out the word that the number should be used only in emergencies."

"All those girls sounded as if they had emergencies," Amanda said. "I couldn't even say hello before they started in on their problems. They couldn't even wait 'til I called Lori to the phone. And it was all about boys, boys, boys!" She pushed the bowl of cereal back almost to the center of the table. "Remind me to skip those years when I get to them," she added in a peculiarly adult tone.

"Amanda, stop playing with your breakfast and eat it." Mrs. Kennedy reached for the toast. "And I'm sure your teen years are going to be just as much fun as Lori's," she added.

"What fun is *she* having?" Amanda asked under her breath.

"Don't be fresh," Mrs. Kennedy warned.

"I'm not being fresh. I'm just asking an honest question."

"Okay, enough, Amanda."

Amanda scowled and finally attacked her bowl of cornflakes.

"You aren't eating, either?" Mrs. Kennedy asked her older daughter. "And you can't tell me you've got so much homework that you have to study at the breakfast table."

Lori's eyes moved up from her lap. "Sorry," she said softly. "It's not really homework, anyway."

"You know how your father feels about reading while we have meals. He's going to be downstairs any minute now."

"I'm not reading," Lori said defensively.

"Then what are you looking at?"

Amanda abandoned her cereal and craned her neck to see what was in her sister's lap. "It's just pictures," she said, crinkling her nose disdainfully. "Dumb pictures of Lori when she was my age."

Mrs. Kennedy's face lit up with surprise. "Whatever made you want to look at old photographs this morning?" she asked in mild amusement.

"They're from camp," Lori said in explanation, moving the pictures up onto the table.

"Camp! My, that was a long time ago. What were you, eleven that summer? That's over five years ago. Let me see them, honey." Mrs. Kennedy drew the pictures to her side of the table. "Oh, look at how cute you were with that long, straight hair," she exclaimed. "And there's the skinny little boy with all the curls that you used to write letters to."

"You used to write letters to little boys when you were my age?" Amanda asked incredulously. "No wonder you get all those phone calls. You started kind of young with all that stuff, didn't you?"

"Amanda, eat your cornflakes," said Mrs. Kennedy. She looked again at the photographs. "I wonder whatever happened to that darling little boy."

"He grew up," Lori said.

"Yes, dear, I realize that. I just wonder what he's doing now, where he is. We always thought you two were fated for each other," she said with a motherly smile.

"He's here," said Lori.

"Here!"

"He goes to Lincoln High."

"Are you serious?"

"I ran into him yesterday in the cafeteria."

"Lori, that's wonderful! What's he like now?"

"Taller." She paused. "A lot taller."

"That's all?"

"Well, he's older, I guess. Sort of."

"So are you, honey."

"Mother, you've got that funny look on your face."

"What funny look, baby?"

"That matchmaking look we all know and love."

"Don't you want me to have any fun watching you grow up?" Mrs. Kennedy laughed.

Footsteps could be heard on the stairway, and a moment later Lori's father appeared. He paused at the door and smiled. "Correct me if I'm wrong, but I do believe that blasted phone hasn't rung for the last fifteen minutes."

"Give it a few more seconds," Amanda said.

She was right. In half a minute it was ringing once again.

Lori didn't know why she had agreed to help the other girls. She had no secret knowledge about girl-boy relationships that they didn't possess themselves. But they wouldn't believe her.

She had handed out advice reluctantly at first. Total honesty had worked with Barry Jensen, so she prescribed that in most cases. Where things seemed more complicated, her advice got more complex.

She already sensed that she shouldn't be meddling at all, but the girls were so eager for her help that she felt she couldn't turn them down. She had never been the center of such attention in her life and she was enjoying the fact that she had conquered Lincoln High so easily. Of course, it had all been an accident, but was she to blame for that?

As she entered the schoolyard and headed toward the main door she spotted Janis waiting for her.

"I'm putting your plan into action today," the girl said enthusiastically. "And I can't wait for the positive results!"

"Janis, you might not get any positive results."

"Sure I will. Look at what you did for Laura. She's in seventh heaven."

"But . . ."

"But nothing. We can all tell you really know guys. Now, when you talk to John Kane today, be sure to—"

"I'm not talking to John Kane today!"

"But you have to. Isn't that part of your magic? You size up the guy and put in a few good words and then the rest is—"

"Wait a minute! I may have given you some advice on how to—"

"Oh, okay. You don't have to talk to him yet. It might not be necessary, anyway. You've given us all confidence, and that's what counts. Confidence, plus your secret knowledge of the workings of the human heart."

"Janis, I don't have any—"

"Oh, stop being so modest! Although maybe

that's why we like you so much. You don't lord it over us that you're so much more experienced." Janis looked at Lori with worshipful eyes. "One day you're going to have to tell us all about how you acquired such wisdom."

Lori suddenly wished she hadn't come to school that day. She didn't have much experience at all. She hadn't even had a real boyfriend. In fact, up to this point in her life, the boy she had been closest to was Ian Winslow, and that had been five years ago when she was eleven and he was twelve. It could hardly have been described as a real romance.

She dreaded the day ahead, but Janis was already tugging her by the elbow into the building. Lori took one last look at the blue fall sky and was certain that by afternoon dark clouds would be forming, ready to crash down all around her when it was time to leave again.

But by afternoon the clouds had failed to materialize. In fact, the sky appeared even bluer, and the corridors of Lincoln High were echoing with the triumphant results of Lori Kennedy's magical advice.

Janis Jamison had shyly told John Kane that she liked the way his sweater fit, and now she had a date for Saturday night.

Jennifer Logan, on the other hand, had boldly told Andy Lawrence that she hated the music he chose on the cafeteria jukebox. Now she had a date for Friday night, during which he planned to convince her that his musical taste had merit.

Sally Landis was going to a tennis tournament

with Rick Johnson—a natural turn of events once she let it be known that she thought team sports were boring.

Those who hadn't had their wishes fulfilled completely were sure that that evening or the next day would bring them happiness, too, and as Lori stood by her locker trying to remember the combination of the lock without looking at the slip of paper in her wallet, she felt both relieved and somewhat proud of herself.

Maybe she did possess secret knowledge that she wasn't even aware of herself.

"You seem to be a star attraction around here," she heard a voice say behind her.

She turned to find Ian leaning against one of the lockers. He was gazing at her with curiosity, his eyes full of questions.

"Hi," she said, wondering whether she was starting to blush. "How come I didn't see you in the halls today?"

"Maybe because you were surrounded all the time by groups of girls blocking your view. I seemed to be passing you between every class, but I guess you didn't have a second to look up."

Lori smiled with embarrassment. "It got a bit out of hand at times, didn't it," she laughed.

"What is this incredible potion you're handing out? Maybe I should be standing in line myself."

"It's nothing, really. Just some old-fashioned common sense."

"That supposedly works miracles," Ian said. "According to the grapevine around here, you've suddenly rearranged the entire social calendar of

Lincoln High. I have a feeling even the guys are going to start cornering you for advice in the near future."

Lori turned back to the locker and fumbled with the dial until she got it open. She definitely was blushing now.

"So I guess a lot *has* happened since arts and crafts camp," Ian said.

She didn't respond to his sentence. Instead she started pulling her jacket from the locker.

"*Has* a lot happened?" he finally asked.

She turned and faced him. "Hasn't a lot happened to you, too?" she asked. "I mean, five years is five years." She didn't know why her voice sounded so brittle. "Like, how come you're staying away from art classes when you have a real talent in that direction?"

"*Do* I have a real talent in that direction?" he asked somewhat coldly, his blue eyes losing their brightness.

"You did when I knew you."

"All those many years ago, you mean. Maybe talents fall by the wayside."

"Or get deliberately lost," Lori said.

"Now why would someone deliberately lose a talent?" Ian mused. "Could it be that a talent might get in the way of other things? Like a normal, healthy adolescence, for instance?" He paused and the muscles in his face suddenly went slack. "What is this weird conversation we're having?" he asked, his smile returning. "I tracked you down to find out when I can see you, not to get into heavy subjects like this."

She couldn't help smiling back at him. "When do you want to see me?" she asked, pulling on her jacket.

"What are you doing tonight?"

Lori laughed. "Homework, I guess."

"Which will be done by when?"

She shrugged. "Eight o'clock if I eat an early dinner."

"You want to meet somewhere?"

"Why don't you come over to my place? That way I won't have to go through any hassle with my parents about going out on a school night. Besides, my mom would like to see you again."

"She would?"

"She has fond memories of you as a skinny little kid."

"You think she'll like me as much now that I'm a big skinny kid?"

"She might."

"It's worth a risk, huh?"

"I think so."

"And what about your advice-to-the-lovelorn service?" he asked. "Won't all your clients be interrupting us with urgent pleas for help?"

"I'll tell them that I'm on vacation."

"In other words, away on a trip."

"A trip?"

Ian's smile broadened. "To the past. When every day was camp and sunshine and good times."

Lori began buttoning up her jacket.

"Gee, it's good to see you!" Ian said with enthusiasm. "It's been much too long—"

Lori glanced at him. His blond curls were bobbing happily against the side of his head, bobbing just the way they used to five years ago when he got excited about something, and his eyes were catching reflections from the lights overhead, just the way they used to from the nightly campfire back then.

Yes, it had been much too long—but could one ever recapture the past? Somehow she felt that things might be a good deal more complicated now that she and Ian had found each other again.

3

Amanda continued to press her face against the glass. "He's a *lot* taller, isn't he?"

"Amanda, get away from the window," Mrs. Kennedy said, not looking up from the piece of needlepoint canvas in her lap.

"A *lot, lot* taller."

"Amanda, don't you have something to do upstairs?" Lori asked.

"Isn't his hair kind of long for these days? I mean even rock stars don't necessarily have—"

"Amanda!" Mrs. Kennedy said sharply. "Stop embarrassing your sister and go find something to do."

"I'm not embarrassing her. I'm just getting everyone prepared for his arrival. I mean, I don't want you to be shocked when you open the door and discover he's a completely different person from the little kid in those pictures."

"He's not a completely different person," Lori said. "Mom will recognize him immediately, so just go find something to do."

"But I want to meet him! I sort of like the way his hair looks. I mean, it's definitely not a boring look. It's more interesting than the short way Lori has hers cut."

"Amanda . . . !" Mrs. Kennedy's voice hinted of dire consequences if Amanda didn't move away from the window. "Be good and go check my yarn box and see if I've got any magenta left."

"Magenta?"

"Yes, like this," Mrs. Kennedy said, holding up a strand of yarn.

"That's magenta?"

Mrs. Kennedy nodded.

"You learn something every day, don't you," Amanda said, starting to move slowly into the hallway. Her journey was interrupted by the sound of the doorbell. "I'll get it!" she yelled, her feet suddenly alive with energy.

Mrs. Kennedy and Lori both looked at each other, letting out a collective sigh that quickly turned to laughter.

"You sure have changed," they heard Amanda saying. "I mean not so much that we wouldn't know you from your pictures, but you're a *lot* taller. Of course I guess I didn't know you back then. Or maybe I did, but I probably wasn't paying attention. I mean, I was born and everything, so they must have brought me along when they picked Lori up at camp. But it wasn't like real camp, was it? I mean I guess it was okay if you like that kind of stuff, but—"

"Amanda, I thought you were on your way to check on my yarn," Mrs. Kennedy said, coming into the hallway.

"Someone had to open the door," Amanda said crossly. "If we waited for you guys to do it, he'd still be standing out on the steps wondering if we were home or not."

"Magenta, darling. And be sure to check all the way through to the bottom." Mrs. Kennedy turned toward the door. "Hello, Ian," she said with a smile. "I hope Amanda hasn't overwhelmed you with her greeting. She's definitely at an overwhelming stage."

"Well, someone in this family has to be outgoing," Amanda muttered as she made her way back down the hall.

Ian smiled at Mrs. Kennedy. *"Did* I ever meet her before?" he asked.

"No, I think we left her at her grandparents the day we picked Lori up from camp. We probably sensed that we wouldn't have been able to pry her away if we'd brought her along. She had a strong mind of her own even back then."

"I see," Ian said, laughing.

"Come on in. Lori's in the living room."

"No, I'm not."

Mrs. Kennedy turned to find her older daughter standing right behind her. "Well, I guess she's not." Mrs. Kennedy laughed. "Why don't we all go back there and try to catch up on everything that's happened to you since that memorable summer you spent at camp."

Lori cleared her throat. "I thought while there's still some light I might show Ian the . . . the things out back."

"The things out back?"

"You know. The garage and the trees and the other stuff," she said weakly.

"The garage? There's nothing very interesting about the garage, baby. And there's all that old junk in there that still needs cleaning out."

"Ian might be interested in that old junk. He might be able to use it."

Mrs. Kennedy frowned. "Use it?"

"For some sort of art project," Lori said quickly.

Mrs. Kennedy turned her frown toward Ian.

"Yes, she's probably right," he said. "You never know what might come in handy these days. Old tires maybe. You can do lots with them if you put your mind to it."

"I don't think there are any old tires in the garage," Mrs. Kennedy said, glancing toward the window. "And it's really not going to be light for much longer. Wouldn't you two rather—" She broke off in midsentence and was suddenly laughing. "I'm being dense, aren't I," she said, her eyes moving from one to the other. "Okay, run along and have some time together. But be sure and come back and at least fill me in on some of the details of the last five years before you leave."

* * *

"Your mom's not that bad," Ian said, leaning back against the discarded refrigerator.

Lori sighed. "No, I guess she's not that bad. We get along really well, except when she . . ."

"Well, at least she's taking an interest. I sometimes wonder if my parents . . . but then, that's another story, and besides, we're not here to discuss the present, are we?"

"We aren't?"

"No, we're here to remember the good times."

Lori felt her heart sink. "You mean the days at camp?" she asked, not bothering to hide her lack of enthusiasm for the subject.

"You don't have incredible memories of those days?" Ian brought his arm up to the top of the refrigerator and traced a line in the dust with his finger. "Remember those mornings when we used to go down to the lake at dawn and try to draw it with that awful chalk that kept crumbling and ruining all our efforts?"

"You consider that part of the good times? Those pictures were terrible."

"I know, but the time we spent making them was wonderful, wasn't it?"

Lori shrugged, her eyes moving up to the loft above them.

"I sure thought you were enjoying those times back then."

"That was back then," she said, arching her neck to peer into the grayness above the ladder.

Ian pulled his lanky body away from the old refrigerator and wiped his hands on the back of his blue jeans. "You don't seem to be in a very good mood tonight," he said.

She didn't say anything, her eyes continuing to stare upward.

"Are you really looking at something, or are you just trying to avoid my gaze?" he asked, moving closer to her.

"There are boxes up there that we've never opened since we've moved here," she said, her foot already on the first rung of the ladder.

"Won't it be too dark to see anything?"

"Not if you hand me that light."

Lori pointed to the fixture hanging against the near wall. Ian took it down from its hook and handed it to her, then stood at the foot of the ladder and watched as she ascended to the overhanging loft. Once she was up there, she switched on the light, flooding the darkness above with a yellowish glow.

"Anything good?" he asked.

"Aren't you coming up?" She was already rummaging through one of the cartons. "Who knows what buried treasure may be waiting to be discovered."

"Buried junk, most likely," Ian said with a laugh that seemed forced.

"Come on up and help me."

He climbed the ladder slowly, as if his long legs didn't trust the wooden crossbars. "You know I'm not really in need of any material for art projects," he said as he stepped onto the platform.

"Maybe we'll find something that will spark your imagination. Like these," she said, turning and holding up some old magazines. "You could use them for collages."

"I don't make collages," he said, sitting down beside her on the wooden planks.

"Well, maybe you should start."

"I told you before. I haven't been into that kind of thing lately."

"Then what have you been into lately?"

She pivoted so that they were facing each other. She had hung the electric lamp on a nail on the wall behind him, and the gold of its glow was moving through his hair, causing the curls to shimmer with highlights. His face was hidden in the shadows, but she could sense that he was uncomfortable. He rested his hands against his knees and said nothing.

"Am I asking questions I shouldn't be asking?" she said.

"No, you can ask anything you want. It's just that I wasn't expecting this. I thought we were going to spend tonight—"

"Reliving the past?" she finished, looking away and pulling one of the boxes closer to her side.

"What's wrong with that?"

"Nothing," she said coolly.

Ian sighed. "You *are* in a strange mood tonight, aren't you?"

"Hey, look at this!" She pulled a floppy black hat from the box. "This isn't in bad shape at all."

"Try it on," he said with sudden eagerness.

Lori held it up to her head and then hesitated. "I'll just disappear in it," she said, laughing and sleeking down her short brown locks. "It would look a lot better on you."

"I'd probably look like an old hillbilly in it!" he protested.

"We'll never know until we try it on you," she said.

For a moment she thought his arms were going to rise up in protest and stop her from placing the hat on him, but as her hands reached over, he held his head perfectly still and let her pull the hat over his curls and then adjust it.

She leaned back and eyed him critically. "Actually, it looks quite dashing," she said.

"You mean I look like a dashing hillbilly," he said laughingly, his hand tugging at one side of the brim.

"You don't look like a hillbilly at all. What you really look like is . . ." Her mouth threatened to go dry.

"Is what?"

"You look like an artist," she managed to get out.

"I thought artists wore berets."

"You know what I mean."

He looked down and suddenly pulled the hat off and tossed it back in the box. "I wish you'd drop this campaign," he said.

"What campaign?"

"To force me back into an old concept you once had of me."

"To force you back! I'm not the one who's intent on bringing back the past and turning us into the great pals we once were for a summer. If anyone's trying to force things back, it's you!"

They stared at each other for a few seconds. She

couldn't find anything in his eyes now. All expression seemed to have been frozen out of the blueness, and she felt her own eyes take on an equivalent iciness.

"Maybe we should go back to the house," she said. "My mother really does want to talk to you."

He flipped down the top of the box containing the hat. "Yeah, maybe that's a good idea," he said, tapping the cardboard with his fingers before drawing his hand away. He stared at the carton for a moment with an intensity that Lori found unsettling. Then he swung his legs over the side of the loft and got a foothold on the ladder. "I think we'll both feel better once we have our feet firmly on the ground," he said, trying to smile.

Lori watched as he disappeared, watched until the last golden curl of his hair had vanished from her sight. She felt a shiver run down her back. What had she been trying to do by bringing him up there and putting that hat on him? She was beginning to act as idiotically as some of the girls who sought her advice at school. Just what had she been trying to prove?

It had certainly been the wrong way to get him to start thinking of her as more than just his pal from summers ago. If she seriously wanted him to . . . The shiver down her back disappeared, and she was suddenly aware of a flush spreading across her face. If she seriously wanted what?

"Are you coming down, or am I supposed to go and talk to your mother alone?"

His question did nothing to stop her mind from

racing. His words came up to her and she understood them, but she didn't offer a response.

"Hey! Did you find some real treasure up there or have you fallen asleep?"

She was far from asleep. Her mind had never been so alive, so totally aware of things. That was what was so awful.

"Come on, Lori. Stop playing games and get down here!"

She switched off the lamp and moved toward the edge of the loft, slowly positioning her body so that she wouldn't have to look down at him. Her feet found the first rung of the ladder, but as she began to descend she must have made a mistake in judgment because suddenly she was sliding, her legs kicking at air and the swift pull of gravity tearing her fingers from the wood. For one agonizing moment her body tensed in anticipation of a painful landing on the garage floor, but in the next second her fall was broken.

"Hey, are you okay?"

He must have been standing directly at the base of the ladder. How else could he have caught her so easily, his long arms reaching out to cushion her rapid descent and draw her against his chest.

"I'm fine," she said in a dazed voice. She began to make tentative attempts to free herself from his grip, but his arms were holding her tightly.

"You're not fine," he said, looking down at her. "There's a nasty scrape on your elbow."

Lori twisted her arm so that she could see it better. "It's not even bleeding," she said.

"The other one, you idiot. I'd better get you back to the house and let your mother look at it." Ian began moving across the garage floor with her still in his arms. "And the next time, look down before you start using a ladder."

She felt a flash of anger run through her. "Accidents can happen, you know," she said with a huffiness that she immediately regretted. Her voice sounded exactly like Amanda's at its most annoying. "And I can still walk perfectly well," she added, the tone of her voice continuing to embarrass her as she tried to gain control of it.

She pushed at his chest and was surprised when this time he readily allowed her to regain a standing position. It was only then that she experienced the pain in her lower leg.

"You're not okay at all, are you?" he said with concern.

"I'm fine!"

She turned and began moving toward the garage door, desperately trying not to wince as her bruised skin chafed against the inside of her pants leg.

"Would you just slow down and let me help you back to the house?" he demanded, coming up from behind and bringing her to a standstill by grabbing her shoulders. "You must have knocked against the side of the ladder or something."

"It's nothing serious."

"Why don't we let your mother be the judge of that?"

Before she could protest, Ian had picked her up once again.

All the way back to the house in the dark, fight it as she might, Lori could not help being conscious of the sensation of having his arms around her.

"You'll be black and blue for awhile," Mrs. Kennedy said, rolling down the leg of Lori's slacks, "but you'll survive." She inspected the bandaged elbow. "And that isn't too bad, either. You're lucky Ian was there to catch you. That garage floor is made of very hard concrete."

Lori stared down at the kitchen floor tile, unable to look Ian in the face. The moments after her fall in the garage had been bad enough, but now the situation seemed impossible, with her mother treating her like a little girl once again.

"So your father's been transferred back to this area," Mrs. Kennedy said, shifting her eyes to Ian. "It certainly is a wonderful coincidence that you and Lori ended up in the same high school."

"It sure is," he said, his smile losing some of its usual shyness.

"I often wondered what happened to that little boy from camp," Mrs. Kennedy continued. "Now I see he's grown up into a fine young man."

Lori groaned inwardly and kept staring down at her leg. She felt an overwhelming sense of relief when she heard a rush of footsteps coming down the hallway. Amanda ran into the room carrying a paper bag.

"No pistachio!" she announced loudly. "Just lots and lots of fudge ripple. I hope nobody minds lots and lots of fudge ripple. Daddy wanted to add some boring vanilla, but I talked him out of it. If we're going to celebrate we might as well really celebrate, don't you think."

"You got nothing but fudge ripple?" Mrs. Kennedy sighed.

"There wasn't any pistachio," Amanda said again. She was already climbing onto a stepstool and reaching for a stack of bowls. "The man said the ice cream shipment went bad. But the fudge ripple arrived in perfect condition, so that's what we got. You'll like it. It's real swirly and interesting. It's definitely not boring to look at or to taste." Amanda shot them a smile over her shoulder. "We got free samples 'cause I was taking so long to make up my mind. That's a good trick to remember for the next time."

Lori risked looking up. Her eyes immediately locked with Ian's and their laughter exploded at the same time.

Amanda paused with the bowls still in midair. "What's so funny?" she asked.

Both shrugged and then broke out laughing once again.

Amanda turned to her mother. "Did I miss something while Dad and I were out getting the ice cream?"

"Oh, there was lots of excitement," Mrs. Kennedy said with a grin.

The eleven-year-old glanced around the kitchen in disbelief. "Excitement?" she said. "Excitement here?"

Lori held up her bandaged elbow and Amanda's eyes widened.

"Wow!" she said. And then she proceeded to punctuate her reaction by dropping one of the bowls.

"I hope it wasn't that awful," Lori apologized as she and Ian stood outside on the front sidewalk.

"Awful! It was great!"

"You've got to be kidding. You mean it was great when my mother started asking you about—"

"I like your mother, Lori," Ian interrupted. "She's friendly and easy to talk to."

"And inquisitive."

"Stop being so rough on her. If you only knew how some girls' mothers treat a guy when he shows up at their homes. Let's face it, they don't usually celebrate by sending out for fudge ripple ice cream," he said laughingly.

"We're going to be eating fudge ripple for the rest of our lives."

"Then maybe you'll have to invite me over again to help you get rid of it."

"What do you think my mother was doing as she walked you to the door?" Lori said. "She practically invited you to come back for breakfast to finish it off."

"She did not!"

"Well, Amanda sure was hinting that it would go great with waffles."

"She might just be right about that."

"But for breakfast?"

"Sounds good to me," he said. "Sounds hilariously wonderful, in fact," he added with a laugh.

The only illumination on the sidewalk came from

a street lamp in front of the next house. It splashed softly across his face, a face that at the moment still held a great many reminders of the twelve-year-old boy she had known in camp.

"Penny for your thoughts," he said, his laughter dying away.

"I don't have any worth buying."

"Not even some about me?"

She looked up at his face, expecting to find a teasing smile, but his expression was one of complete seriousness.

"No comment, huh?" He still didn't smile.

Lori became painfully aware of the silence of the street and the futile attempts of a slight breeze in the treetops to bring things back to noisy life.

"You still in pain?" Ian asked.

"Pain?" She responded too loudly, her voice echoing across the darkness of the lawn.

"I guess it will be worse in the morning," he said.

"I didn't hurt myself that much. I'll be perfectly fine in the morning."

He didn't say anything, but he was looking directly down into her face. Even in the dim light, the irises of his eyes were extraordinarily blue. She found herself having to look away.

"I hear they still need people for that decorating committee," he said.

Lori nodded, grateful for a new topic of conversation.

"Someone to hang streamers, maybe?"

"You could do a lot more than hang streamers."

He raised his pale eyebrows in warning. "I could also refuse to volunteer my services completely."

"Is that what you're doing? Volunteering your services?"

"I was considering the possibility." A smile began to form on his lips but didn't quite make it. "Or wouldn't that be pleasing to you?" he asked.

"To me?"

"I get the feeling that at times you're not too crazy about me."

She looked down at the grass.

"I guess maybe it was too much to expect to pick up from where we left off after all these years, wasn't it?" Ian continued. "There's been some water under the bridge, so to speak."

Lori looked up. "Ian, I—"

"No, that's okay." He managed to twist his lips into an approximation of a smile. "I should have realized that it might be like starting over again."

Lori felt herself brightening at his words. Maybe there *was* a chance that . . .

"I guess a real friendship sometimes takes a while to rebuild," he added.

She felt her heart sink.

Friendship. Friends. How she hated all words like that at the moment. Couldn't he begin to see that there were other possibilities?

"I think I will sign up for that committee," he said, drawing up to his full height. "It will probably be a good way to get involved in the extracurricular world of Lincoln. Do I have to go see a particular person or do I just show up at the next meeting?"

"Just come to the next meeting," she said. "There's one tomorrow afternoon."

"So soon?"

"We've got lots of work to do."

"Okay, then, I'll see you there."

Lori nodded.

"And tell your mom I'm willing to come over anytime and help finish up that fudge ripple."

"I'll tell her," she said.

Ian looked as if he was about to turn, but he hesitated. Lori was surprised when his hand reached out slowly and touched her upper arm. His fingers gave her a gentle squeeze, the warmth of his touch staying with her after he moved his arm away.

"Take care of yourself," he said. "And try to avoid ladders for the rest of the night. I'll see you tomorrow." He began to turn away and then stopped to grin at her, "Remember, lights out in all cabins at ten on the dot. And no flashlights under the covers."

Lori watched him walk down the sidewalk, the gray shadows of the leaf-heavy trees plunging his figure into pools of darkness from which he would emerge at intervals, his blond curls momentarily capturing the hazy light of the street lamps as his long strides propelled him forward. Finally the night swallowed him completely, and there was nothing for her to gaze at but the deserted suburban street.

Lori turned toward her house. Did she really want to go inside? She still had to finish some homework, but as she began walking toward the front door, she wondered if she would be able to deal with algebraic equations that night.

"Phone call!" Amanda's voice shouted at her

from the living-room window. "Some dumb girl about you-know-what!"

Lori found herself quickening her pace.

Someone else's problems. Someone else's life that needed sorting out. That would be a lot easier to concentrate on tonight.

She pulled open the door with surprising eagerness.

Someone else's problems.

And then maybe she'd be ready for the algebraic ones.

And then . . . and then it would be time for . . . for *lights out in all cabins at . . .*

Her sigh sounded down the hallway as she ran toward the phone.

4

I nominate Lori Kennedy!" Janis Jamison's voice boomed out across the art room.

Lori's head suddenly cleared of all other thoughts as she heard her name being spoken loudly. She hadn't been concentrating at all on the meeting, and now suddenly she was the focus of everyone's attention.

"Yes, let's have Lori," Jennifer Logan said. "We need someone with her know-how."

Lori looked up at the blackboard at the front of the room. Mrs. Rinehart was standing there holding a piece of chalk in midair. On the board itself was a list of decorating assignments. All had names written next to them except for the one entitled "Entrance."

Lori glanced at Janis, hoping her new friend would give her some kind of clue as to what such an assignment involved. Janis's eyes were too busy darting up and down the rows of seats, taking pleasure in the stir her nomination had caused.

"Yeah, give it to Lori," a short boy at a front desk said, turning to stare back at her. "She could just *stand* at the entrance. That would be decoration enough in my book."

Mrs. Rinehart rapped the end of her piece of chalk against the blackboard. "Ladies and gentlemen," she said sternly. "Aren't we forgetting the basic rules of parliamentary procedure?"

A series of sighs, punctuated by some laughter, could be heard throughout the room.

"I thought we'd agreed that the only way to run this committee this year was by the rules." Mrs. Rinehart crossed her arms and frowned at the students seated in front of her. "Now let's try to remember that." She turned back to the blackboard. "The name of Lori Kennedy has been put into nomination. Do I hear a seconding motion?"

"We don't need to bother with seconding," Janis said. "We don't even need to vote. We all agree, Mrs. Rinehart."

Mrs. Rinehart didn't seem to be listening. "Does anyone here second the nomination?"

There were more sighs in the room, but Jennifer Logan began clearing her throat. As she did so, the door of the classroom pushed open and everyone's heads turned.

Lori felt a great sense of relief as the blond curls appeared. She hadn't seen Ian all day, and when he had failed to show up at the committee meeting, she had begun to assume he'd decided not to join the decorating committee after all. Smiling apologetically, he maneuvered his lanky frame down the aisle to the back of the classroom.

"Sorry," he murmured to Lori as he dropped into the seat behind her. "I got trapped into helping someone from Visual Aids lug a projector up to the second floor. We had a minor accident on the way." He held up a bandaged finger and then glanced at Lori's elbow. "How are your war wounds today?" he asked.

The sound of chalk tapping against the blackboard could be heard once again.

"I presume we'd all like to get home this afternoon," Mrs. Rinehart said with undisguised annoyance. "Let's try to get on with this final nomination."

"Nomination for what?" Ian whispered.

"For Lori to be in charge of the entrance decorations," Janis replied without lowering her voice. "We're going to have to go through the whole dumb process instead of just declaring her the winner by acclamation. Mrs. Rinehart is a stickler for following the rules."

"Someone around here has to follow the rules," the teacher said angrily. The class fell completely silent and Janis began sinking guiltily back into her seat. "I don't think it's too much to ask for a seconding of this nomination, now is it?"

The class remained silent, and then Lori saw the blur of Ian's arm as it shot upward.

"I second the nomination," he said in a serious, businesslike tone.

Mrs. Rinehart nodded. "Thank you," she said as

she began writing on the blackboard. "Are there any more nominations?"

Sighs could be heard rising again in the class-room.

"It's by acclamation, Mrs. Rinehart," Janis said wearily. "We don't even need to take a vote."

"Yes, by acclamation," someone else said.

"Yeah, and I second the acclamation!" the short boy in the front seat called out. "Three cheers for Lori and let's hope she's as good at art as she is at advice to the lovelorn!"

"I didn't know you blushed so easily." Ian laughed as they made their way down the hall.

"I'm not blushing."

"Yes, you are. It hasn't left your face since that little guy—"

"Hey, Lori! Where are you rushing off to so fast?" Janis was having trouble holding onto her books as she ran toward them. "I have to talk to you about things."

Lori found herself coming to a reluctant stop. Suddenly she began feeling very tired as the girl rapidly approached.

"Listen," Janis said, practically out of breath. "There's been a little problem with you-know-who. Everything's worked out fine except for—"

Janis' words were choked off in midsentence as her eyes took in Ian's long-limbed body leaning against one of the lockers. Lori had already noticed how Janis tended to become aware of things a bit slowly at times. Obviously her new friend had just realized that Lori wasn't alone.

"What's the matter?" Lori asked.

Janis continued to stare at Ian, holding her gaze for a few seconds more than was necessary.

"Janis?" Lori almost felt like waving a hand in front of the girl's face.

"What?" Janis asked in a softer tone than usual, swinging her head slowly back to Lori's face.

"You said there was a problem with—"

"Oh, it can wait." Out of the corner of her eye Janis continued to observe Ian. "I don't want to be interrupting anything," she added.

"You're not interrupting."

Janis didn't seem to be listening. "It's nothing," she said quietly. "I'll call you later." Her voice was threatening to turn into a mere whisper. "That's probably a better idea."

"Okay," Lori said. "Call me later."

Janis' gaze had turned back completely to Ian once again. "Thanks for seconding my nomination," she said.

Ian nodded.

"It was really nice of you to get me out of my predicament," Janis continued with more animation. "Sometimes I get the feeling that Mrs. Rinehart thinks I'm a little too . . . well, anyway, thanks."

"I was just following the rules of parliamentary procedure," Ian said.

"You follow them really well," Janis said seriously. "Are you going to be working with Lori?"

"If she chooses me."

"Oh, it's not a matter of her choosing you," Janis said. "Everyone gets to sign up for their first choice, and then if too many people want the same committee—well, Mrs. Rinehart sorts it out in the end, but it can get very political."

"Political?" Ian was just this side of laughter and Lori had to swallow to control hers.

"You know," Janis continued in the same serious vein, "if Mrs. Rinehart really likes you, then you can usually talk your way on to the committee of your choice, but if she . . . well, last year I didn't exactly get any plum assignments, but I don't think *you'll* have any trouble. I mean, you followed the rules of parliamentary procedure and everything, and you're so . . . so . . . tall."

The second the word erupted from Janis' mouth, the girl realized how funny it sounded. She couldn't stop ending her sentence with an embarrassed laugh, a laugh that immediately produced similar ones from Ian and Lori. Suddenly there was a much more relaxed feeling among the three of them.

"Oh, you know what I'm trying to say," Janis giggled. "I don't mean that just because you're tall, she'll . . . oh, you know what I mean. Well you do, don't you?" The usual loudness of her voice was returning in all its strength. "Don't just stand there pretending I'm not making any sense!"

"You're making complete sense," Ian answered laughing.

Janis giggled again. "I am?"

"You sure are," Lori said. "Absolutely complete sense."

Janis tried to straighten her lips. "Well, maybe I am," she said, as though talking to herself. "And then maybe it doesn't matter, as long as I hang around with people like you who'll tell me I do, even when the rest of the world seems to think . . . oh, we just all have to end up on this committee together, don't we? I'll just have to make Mrs. Rinehart see that you two can bring out all the potential in me. We'll make that entranceway totally . . . entrancing!"

"Entrancing?" Ian lifted an eyebrow.

"Yes, don't you get it? Entrance. Entrancing."

"What is this girl talking about?" Ian asked Lori.

"Beats me."

"You do, too, get it!" Janis exclaimed, and then burst out into laughter once again. "Stop teasing me. Friends don't tease each other."

"Sure they do," Ian said. He moved away from the locker and stretched to his full height next to Lori. "Don't you agree, Lori?"

"It's that girl again," Amanda yelled down the hallway, not bothering to cover the receiver with her hand. "The one who called half an hour ago and hurt my eardrums."

Lori glared at her younger sister as she took the phone from her hand. The eleven-year-old didn't move from her position next to the table. "A-manda, isn't it time for you to help Mom get ready for dinner?" Lori asked.

"It's early."

"Maybe you could put in a few more minutes perfecting your napkin-folding skills."

"There's nothing wrong with the way I fold napkins!" Amanda said angrily.

"Just go find someplace else to stand, okay?"

Amanda moved away unhappily. "I bet if they held a napkin-folding contest for my age group I'd win hands down," she muttered.

Lori waited for her sister to disappear into the living room before she brought the phone up to her ear.

"Sorry about the delay," she said. "My kid sister's going through a phase."

"Oh, aren't we all," Janis sighed. "Did I really hurt her eardrums?"

"No." Lori laughed.

"Well, my mother tells me that I do tend to talk too loudly at times."

Lori cleared her throat. "So what's the problem with John Kane?" she asked.

"Huh?"

"Isn't that what you're calling about?"

"Oh, we can get to that later."

"We can?"

"Sure. Why don't you tell me about what's-his-name first."

"What's-whose-name?"

"Like how come you weren't home from school when I called earlier? I mean, where did you go and what did you do and what did he say and how'd you get him interested in you so quickly?"

"Are we talking about Ian Winslow?"

"What's-his-name. You know. The guy with the legs and all those blond curls and everything."

"He's just an old friend," Lori said impatiently.

"Sure. Tell me another one."

"That's the truth. We went to summer camp

together a long time ago, and then by sheer chance we both showed up at Lincoln High this fall. That's all."

"Okay, so don't tell me the truth."

"Janis—"

"Well, at least tell me what you did this afternoon. Maybe I can pick up some pointers."

"Wouldn't you rather talk about John Kane?"

"We'll get to that later. How come all of a sudden you've gotten so secretive? Or are you working on some new method you don't want to reveal until it's perfected? Is that it? Is this Ian what's-his-name a real test case for you? Tell me."

"You've got it all wrong, Janis," Lori said.

"Let *me* be the judge of that, okay? Just tell me what you did this afternoon."

"We didn't do anything."

"Oh, come on!"

"I had to go downtown to pick up some school supplies and he had to—"

"You mean you went your separate ways!"

"Yes."

"And that's all?"

"Yes, Janis, that's all."

"You really expect me to believe—"

"Janis, can't we get back to your problems and leave mine alone?" Lori asked with irritation.

There was a moment of silence from the other end of the line. "Oh, no," Janis finally sighed. "You mean you've finally found somebody you don't know how to deal with? You mean with all your expertise and experience, even you can't figure out—"

"I thought you wanted to talk about you-know-who."

"That's a minor matter. Besides, if you're having trouble with . . . I mean, maybe your advice . . . no, I guess not. I guess it would still work on my level, and by the time I get involved with guys like what's-his-name, you'll have perfected your technique and can pass it on to the rest of us."

"Janis, I think my mom's calling me for dinner."

"I didn't hear anybody."

"She talks very softly."

"Well then, can I call you back in an hour?"

"I have lots of homework to—"

"We'll do it together over the telephone. And then you can spare me a few minutes, can't you? Is there any reason why not?"

Janis called back after dinner. They didn't get much homework done over the phone, but Lori managed to deal with Janis's minor problem with John Kane. She also managed to steer the conversation away from the subject of Ian Winslow, though the effort left her exhausted.

She had just settled down into an easy chair in the living room when the telephone rang again. Amanda, trying to put off her usual bedtime, leaped at the opportunity to answer it. She stayed away for several minutes before returning to the living-room door.

"It's for you," she said, nodding vaguely in the direction of Lori. "And it's not one of those girls."

Lori started getting to her feet. "Who is it then?" she asked.

Amanda didn't answer her directly. Instead, the eleven-year-old turned to her mother and said: "How come he wanted to talk to me?" she asked. "He called for Lori, but he wanted to know how I was, too. He really talked to me. Just like I was a real girl instead of just a kid. How come he did that?"

Mrs. Kennedy smiled as she reached for some new yarn. "Maybe he's a nice boy," she said.

"Mother . . ." Lori shot Mrs. Kennedy a warning look as she began heading toward the hall. If only her mother wouldn't keep making comments!

"Hi, it's me."

"So I gathered," she said, leaning against the wall and cradling the receiver between her neck and shoulder. "You really made a big impression on my sister."

"I like kids."

Lori didn't say anything.

"So I guess you're wondering why I'm calling," he said finally.

"You've come up with some terrific ideas for my entrance committee."

"Am I on your entrance committee?"

"I don't know. Maybe you'd better talk to Mrs. Rinehart about it."

"Do you want me on your committee?"

Lori hesitated. "Sure, why not. You're a lot more talented than I am."

"Don't sell yourself so short."

"I'm just stating the truth."

Again there was silence over the line.

"Well, anyway, I was wondering what you were doing tomorrow afternoon."

"There's a committee meeting tomorrow afternoon."

"After that. I was thinking maybe we could go exploring."

"Exploring?"

"Well, since we're both relatively new in this town I thought it might be fun to walk around a bit and get to know it better. And it will give you a chance to escape from all your female advice-seekers."

"Why would I want to escape from them?" Lori asked in a brittle voice that she immediately regretted.

"Aren't they starting to drive you crazy?"

"They're my friends."

"I know, but . . ."

More silence spread from one receiver to the other.

"So, anyway. How about it? You want to try some exploring with your old hiking chum tomorrow?"

"We won't have much time, now that it's getting dark early," Lori pointed out.

"Where's your sense of adventure?" he said with a laugh that she remembered from summers before.

"Oh, all right."

"Such enthusiasm," he said, laughing again. "You used to be crazy about hikes."

"Back when I was a girl you mean."

"You're still a girl, aren't you?"

"I suppose so."

"It'll be fun, so start getting excited!"

"Lori, isn't it time you were in bed?" Mrs. Kennedy was frowning as she stood in the doorway of her daughter's room. "Are you still working on homework?"

Lori looked up from her desk. "I've only got one more problem to finish," she said, poking the open book with her pencil.

"Too many phone calls again tonight, don't you think?"

Lori shrugged. "I'm new in town," she said.

"I know, but still . . ." Mrs. Kennedy leaned against the door frame. "What did Ian want? Or is that a secret?"

"He wants to go exploring tomorrow afternoon."

"Oh. That sounds like fun."

"It sounds like a rerun of summer camp to me," Lori said angrily. She looked down at her algebra book. The print was starting to blur and for a moment she wondered if she was going blind. Then she felt the moisture begin to escape down her cheeks.

"Oh, baby, what's the matter?" Mrs. Kennedy asked, moving into the room.

"Nothing's the matter." Lori gulped.

Mrs. Kennedy reached one hand out to her daughter's head and stroked her hair. "Don't worry, honey. Things have a way of working out," she said.

Lori leaned her head on her mother's arm and let the stroking fingers offer comfort. She didn't care that this was a scene that had been repeated many times in her childhood. All the usual sense of irritation at her mother melted away as the fingers continued to move over her hair.

5

We could all meet out at my house," Janis said, handing the piece of paper back to Lori. "We've got some good people on that list. Once we pool our talents we're bound to come up with some dynamite ideas. And the best place to do that would be my place."

"I thought we were supposed to meet with Mrs. Rinehart in the art room," Lori said, folding the list and putting it into her notebook.

"That's eventually. Next week or something. We can meet out at my place over the weekend."

"Maybe we should meet at my place," said Lori. "Since I'm in charge of the committee, it's probably my responsibility—"

"Don't worry about responsibilities. It's no big deal. In fact my mom loves to have kids come over.

It would be sort of like a party. It wouldn't have to be just people on the decorating committee. I could invite over lots of others and turn it into something special."

"But—"

"No buts about it," Janis said with excitement. "Here, you give that list back to me and I'll tell everyone on it that we're to meet on Saturday night—"

"Saturday night!"

"Saturday night at my place. Stop giving me that funny look. Things will turn out fine. We'll get our plans set and have fun at the same time. Besides, I want you to have a chance to see all the girls and guys interacting so that you can get a better idea of what you're dealing with."

"What do you mean, what I'm dealing with?"

"Just hand me the list," Janis insisted.

Lori did so reluctantly. Mrs. Rinehart had given it to her only minutes before; she hadn't expected to receive it that soon. The teacher had drawn up the subcommittees without any difficulty during the last minutes of the meeting, and only a few students had protested their assignments. Janis must have greatly exaggerated all that business about politicking for positions.

"I guess *you* can tell *him*," Janis said, glancing down the short list. "I arranged it, you know," she added.

"Arranged what?"

"Ian what's-his-name being on our subcommittee. I arranged my being on it too. I got to Mrs.

Rinehart during study hall and told her all about how you were new in town and needed someone like me who knew the ropes to help you out. For some reason she fell for it. And then I hinted that you might quit if what's-his-name didn't get on your list."

"You did not!"

"Sure did! I always look out for my friends."

Lori didn't know whether to groan or laugh.

"How come he disappeared so quickly after the meeting?" Janis asked in as matter-of-fact a voice as she could muster.

"He had to make a phone call."

"What kind of phone call? Yesterday he seemed to want to hang around you and today he's that eager to get away to make a phone call? Did you make a mess of things today, or what?"

Lori didn't want to admit that she had thought it strange when Ian had rushed out of the room so quickly. He had been acting strangely all day. Every time she had seen him in the halls that day he had merely given her a mysterious smile and kept on moving.

"So did you have a fight, or am I misreading the situation completely?" Janis asked, stuffing the list into the middle of a textbook.

"You're misreading it."

"Thank goodness. So I guess you're still busy perfecting your technique and we can all relax." Janis began buttoning her sweater. "Listen, I have to be running. If I'm to organize a big party by Saturday night, I've got to see to lots of things. Just don't forget to invite him, okay? I'll probably talk to you tonight."

Lori began gathering up her books as Janis dashed out of the room. Ian had said that he would be coming back there to pick her up, but she wondered if she might have time to run to her locker and stow away the texts she wouldn't be needing that night. She didn't want to have to carry them along on their outing.

Her eyes traveled to the window. The day hadn't been very sunny, and there was a grayness to the sky beyond the playing field that hinted at more than just the arrival of an early evening. She glanced at her watch. It was only four o'clock.

There was a shuffle of feet at the doorway and then a voice spoke. "Lori?" it asked.

The voice wasn't the one she had expected to hear. She turned from the window to discover a boy of small stature and ample girth looking tentatively into the room.

"You *are* Lori, aren't you?" he asked, not quite looking her in the eye.

Lori nodded.

"Can I . . . can I talk to you?" He didn't wait for her answer. He entered the classroom with a quick glance behind him. As he came in he pulled the door almost completely shut behind him. "This is kind of personal," he said in explanation.

Lori vaguely remembered having seen him in the halls, but she couldn't for the life of her place him.

He must have read her thoughts. "I guess we don't exactly know each other," he said. "I'm

John." For a moment he seemed to be on the point of extending his hand but then obviously decided not to. He continued to hold his arm at an odd angle to his side. "John," he repeated. "John Kane."

Lori felt a smile form across her lips. So this was John Kane, the boy Janis had gotten a date with because of Lori's help. She could see his appeal to Janis almost instantly. It was a case of opposites attracting. John Kane probably never spoke loudly, never rushed headlong into things the way Janis always seemed to be doing.

John still wasn't looking at her directly. "I hear that you've been . . . been sort of . . . sort of helping people out," he said. "Like helping them out with . . . with . . . well, you know. . . ." His eyes went to hers for a brief moment. They were brimming with a strange combination of eagerness and embarrassment. "I know it's not exactly the kind of thing a guy does," he said, looking away again, "but I thought maybe . . . well, since everyone's talking about how you're so smart and everything about . . ." His voice ground to a complete halt.

"You want my advice?" Lori asked, feeling a sinking sensation inside her chest. "Don't you think you should be talking to some guy about this first?"

"No, no guy!" John said rapidly. "I couldn't talk to them about this. It's too . . . too personal."

Lori wasn't sure if she wanted to hear anything too personal from the lips of John Kane. She was burdened down enough with the revelations of a great percentage of the female population of Lincoln High.

"It's just that there's this girl," John said. "I mean I like her a lot and we've already got this date for Saturday night, but . . . well, I've gotten the impression that she thinks this date is going to be a big thing, and . . . well to be perfectly honest, I'm not that great on first dates, and—"

"We're talking about Janis Jamison, aren't we?" Lori said, cutting him off in midsentence.

John looked startled. "You really do know things, don't you?" he said in amazement.

"She's my best friend at Lincoln."

"Oh, I didn't know that. I guess I don't know that much about Janis. She's been around all the time I suppose, but it wasn't until last week that I realized . . . and then a few days ago when she started paying me those compliments and . . . so she's your best friend, huh?"

"Well, I haven't known her that long, but she was the person who tried to make me feel most welcome here."

"Yeah, she's like that."

The conversation suddenly went dead between the two of them.

Lori cleared her throat. "Janis is throwing a big party Saturday night," she said. "I don't think you'll have much to worry about. You'll be with a whole bunch of other people."

"I will? I thought we were just going to the movies."

"There's been a change in plans."

John's face brightened. "I guess this means I won't have to worry about small talk and things like that. I guess this means she'll be kind of busy and I can just sort of get to know her better in little bits. This means that I can . . . hey, thanks for helping me out, Lori!" His eyes were looking excitedly into hers now. "I knew it was a good idea to try and get some advice from you!"

Lori's mouth fell open. "I haven't given you any advice," she said in astonishment. "I just told you that—"

John wasn't listening. "I think some of the other guys around here might want to talk to you, too. We all have problems from time to time and you just might be the best thing that's ever happened to Lincoln High."

"But—"

"Have you been giving Janis advice, too?" he asked, narrowing his eyes slightly. "Is that why all of a sudden I became aware of her?" His face broke into a smile. "Oh, what does it matter, anyway? And now you've gone and arranged this party so that—"

"I didn't arrange any party!"

"Thanks, Lori." John began moving toward the door. "Maybe if I hurry I can catch up with Janis. I think I saw her heading toward the west door a few minutes ago. I can probably take a shortcut through the parking lot and—"

John's head was still turned toward Lori as he reached for the door. It began moving before he made contact with the knob, and he found himself falling forward against another body. "Whoa! Sorry!" he said with embarrassment. He shot a parting look at Lori. "Thanks!" he yelled out and then pushed past the lanky frame of Ian Winslow.

Lori breathed a sigh of relief.

"What was that all about?" Ian asked.

"Oh, nothing," Lori answered, laughing.

"It sure looked like something to me."

"It was nothing. Really. He was under the mistaken impression that I'd just given him some great advice."

"Mistaken impression? You mean he and the rest of the school have been totally duped?" Ian moved slowly down the aisle toward her. "I guess this means you're going to develop a group of male fans, too?"

There was a teasing quality to his voice that Lori wasn't enjoying. "Did you make your important phone call?" she asked, gathering her books together and glancing once again at the scene beyond the window.

"Mission accomplished," Ian replied with a gracefully executed salute. "And now the fun can begin."

"Fun?"

"Yes. Our grand exploration."

"Under darkening skies?" she said, nodding toward the window.

"Darkening skies! Those skies aren't darkening. There's going to be an amazing sunset. All that gray is just camouflage."

"Right."

"No, I have it on the best authority—tonight's sunset is going to be great."

"I'll remember to watch it from my bedroom window," Lori said drily.

"You won't be anywhere near your bedroom when the sun sets."

"Oh, won't I?"

"No. You see, that very important phone call was to your mother. I just told her you wouldn't be showing up for dinner tonight, that you had a change of plans."

"Thanks for letting me in on all of this."

"Don't get in a huff!" said Ian. "I've mapped out the whole route so that we can pick up the pizza just before we get to our destination."

"I didn't know we had a destination. I thought we were just going exploring for an hour or so."

"There's nothing wrong with having a destination, is there?" he asked with a smile.

"Where exactly are we going?"

"When we get there you'll know."

"Supposing I don't like where we're going?"

"Don't worry. It'll have to be great. With you and me and a pizza, any spot has to be great, doesn't it? Now, let's hurry up and get rid of all those books you're holding and get going."

"But I need some of these books for homework tonight."

His eyebrows shot up with exasperation. "Explorers don't even *think* about homework," he said.

"Well, this one does."

"Okay, so you'll lug a few books along. But let's hurry. I don't want to miss that sunset and wind up being stuck out in the middle of nowhere with just a cold pizza and a girl worried about algebra problems. I promise I'll get you home in time to finish whatever you have to finish, but the sun isn't going to wait for us to get into position, and it only gives one performance an evening, so let's get going!"

"Here, take this."

"Ian, where are we really going?" Lori asked, reaching for the cardboard box that he was holding out to her. The smell of the pizza reminded her that she hadn't had anything to eat since an early lunch before chemistry lab. She wished they could stop where they were and at least sample one piece, but ever since they had left the pizza parlor, Ian had been intent on moving down this particular street with increasing speed.

"We're almost there," he said. "I just have to figure out the best way to manage this."

"Manage what?"

"Getting over that wall."

Lori looked to where he was pointing. "Ian," she said with annoyance, "we can't—"

"Why can't we?"

"First of all it would be tres—"

"Only technically speaking," he scoffed. "Real explorers aren't bothered by such technicalities, anyway. And I've been told it's a time-honored tradition to get over that wall."

"Who told you that?" she asked irritably.

"Well, some of the guys were mentioning it the other day, and it sounded really interesting."

"To climb over a ten-foot wall?" she said sarcastically.

"It's not a ten-foot wall," he said with disgust. "And it's what's on the other side that's interesting."

"And just what might that be?"

A mysterious smile appeared on his lips. "I guess you'll never know unless you help me figure out how to scale the wall."

"Can't we just eat the pizza here and rely on our imaginations to—"

"But we won't be able to see the sunset from here."

Lori looked up at the sky. "It's going to be just as gray on the other side of that wall as it is here."

"That's not what I've been told." Ian pointed once again toward the wall. "That isn't the everyday world over there," he said. "That's a magic kingdom."

She glanced at the overgrown foliage shooting up from the top of the stones. "It looks like an abandoned piece of property to me."

"Exactly," Ian said animatedly. "I'm sure the town fathers consider it an ugly eyesore, but to the kids around here it's something else."

"Isn't it getting kind of late in the day for this?" Lori asked. "We've been walking for a couple of hours now. We've covered practically all of Lincoln."

"Which is exactly why we can't quit now. The

tour won't be complete without taking in the Belvedere property," Ian insisted. He was already moving across the patch of dying, uncut grass to the stone wall. "I'll get to the top and then you can hand up the box to me and then . . ." He looked over his shoulder at her and laughed. "Well, we'll figure out something. Besides, we're both in good shape, aren't we? No bandages or anything today."

He didn't have that much trouble getting up the wall once he found footholds on several of the stones where the connecting cement had been chipped away. Once at the top, he beckoned to her to approach and pass up the pizza and her books.

"Now, come on up," he said. "Just do it the way I did."

It wasn't that difficult once her feet found the right places. Someone had obviously chiseled out this route before them. Ian reached down with his hands and drew her up the last few feet with a strength that surprised her.

"Okay," he said, shifting the box containing the pizza to his side and peering down into the mass of bushes below. "Now all we have to do is . . ." He pointed out a heavy branch that looked as though it would hold the weight of one person. "Go ahead," he said. "You used to be a pretty good climber back at camp."

"I haven't climbed a tree in years," she said.

"Then maybe it's about time you did. Go on. Let's see if you still remember how to do it. Don't worry. If you get stuck I'll give you some pointers."

"I don't need any pointers," she said. She moved

along the branch quickly and dropped to the ground. Looking up at him, she smiled. "Now it's your turn," she said.

"You have to take this first." He held out the cardboard pizza box.

"Hand it down," she said, moving closer to the wall. "Maybe you'd better turn it vertically," she suggested.

"No, then the pizza would stick to the top of the box and be a complete mess. Just move a little nearer and I'll balance myself with my other arm and—"

The box slipped at the same time that he did. She tried in vain to catch the pizza, but it fell against the wall and then to the ground a few feet away. Ian landed right at her feet, the entire length of his body suddenly stretched out before her, his head cushioned at an angle by a nearby bush.

"Ian, are you okay?" she asked anxiously, leaning down and moving her hand to his shoulder. She could sense panic rising in her voice. "Ian?" she said, shaking him gently. "Ian?"

A short moan came from his lips and then he slowly lifted his head. "Where am I?" he murmured.

"You're here with me," she said, relief flooding her body.

He started to sit up, turning his head from side to side. "Here? Where's here?" Then he looked at Lori. "Ah!" he said. "In the magic kingdom with the fairy princess!"

"Ian," she said, her relief shot through with

annoyance, "stop acting silly. That fall really gave me a scare."

He brought his hand up to his tangled hair and brushed away some dead leaves that were clinging to the curls. "What do you think it did to me?" he said with a half-smile.

"Are you sure you're okay?" she asked.

He began to get to his feet. "I'm fine," he said, shaking off some of the patches of dirt clinging to his clothes.

"Here, let me do that," she said.

The soil was dry and dusty and fell away easily. "There, that's better," she said, stepping back and checking to see if she had missed any patches. "But are you sure you didn't break anything?"

Ian pushed his arms up above his head and stretched them as high as they would go. "No, I may have a few bruises tomorrow morning, but other than that, I'll survive." He looked directly into her eyes. "You know, we've got to stop repeating these patterns," he said.

"Patterns?"

"First you fell. Then me. We should at least try to do these things together the next time. You still hungry?" he asked, breaking the gaze and shifting his eyes to the cardboard box next to the wall.

"Starving," she admitted, happy with the change of subject.

"Maybe we'd better . . ." He bent over and pulled at the top of the box. "Then again . . ." He opened it further so that she could see the inside. The elements of the pizza seemed to have separated, the tomato sauce and cheese sticking to the roof of the container, while the dough sat alone at the bottom. The mushrooms were plastered to the sides of the box.

"It looks like a build-your-own-pizza kit," Ian said, laughing. "All we have to do is fit it together. You want to try?"

Lori reached down and touched the crust. "It's getting really cold and hard," she said.

He pushed his finger through the sauce and cheese and lifted it to his lips. "Doesn't taste that bad," he commented. "Then again, it doesn't taste that great, either."

"Maybe we should go back and get another one," she suggested.

He reached in his pocket and came up with a little bit of change. "Have you got any money on you?"

"Enough for a pizza," she said. "Why don't we go back to that place and eat there and then call it a day. I really do have homework to do." She glanced at the top of the wall and could just make out the edges of her books.

"Don't you want to see the rest of the magic kingdom?" Ian asked.

"It's just an abandoned estate, isn't it?" she said. "What is there? An old house and the grounds? It doesn't sound that magical to me."

"But there's the lookout point!" he exclaimed, the excitement returning to his voice.

"What lookout point?"

"Come on and I'll show you. I'm sure we can

find it. I got detailed directions from one of the guys."

"Ian, it's getting late, and we have to get back over that wall, and my books are still on top, and . . ."

Ian shook his head in dismay. "Where's the old Lori who was game for anything?" he asked. "Does nothing excite her except handing out advice and meddling in the lives of—"

"I'm not meddling! I'm simply—"

"Okay, okay. I'll drop the subject. But please just come with me and try to find the lookout point."

He held out his hand and she let him take hers, despite the anger that his earlier words had provoked. They moved through the bushes and trees toward more open ground, and she tried to enjoy the moment for what it was, for the pleasure of his long fingers laced warmly through hers.

"We can skip the mansion," he said, nodding towards the fire-gutted foundation. "Now all we have to do is find the path leading down to the . . ."

That proved harder to do than he had expected. There were many paths beyond the house and all of them seemed to be going off in the same direction into a wooded section. Only as they began taking them did they discover that most circled right back to the point where they had started.

"How about this one?" he said, pointing down the next path they came to. Lori craned her neck and tried to decide whether it would repeat the pattern of the others. She shrugged, and Ian laughed and gave her hand a tug. "Come on, we'll try them all, and the sunset will just have to wait for us to find it."

Lori looked up at the sky. It was slate gray now and in half an hour she was certain it would be dark.

The path began twisting like the others, but just as it seemed to be turning back toward the mansion it straightened once again, and suddenly they were standing on a different section of lawn. And down below them, at the bottom of a steep incline, was a small gazebo—and beyond that a vista that Lori didn't think existed in Lincoln.

"This is it!" Ian said, pulling her along as he ran through the untrimmed grass to the open, roofed pavilion jutting out from the side of the hill. Despite some peeling paint, the gazebo was in remarkably good shape, its delicate ornamentation disguising its solid construction. Ian ran headlong up the small flight of steps and onto the firm wooden flooring, drawing Lori along with him.

The town itself was spread out below, its rooftops peeking through the hundreds of trees that lined the streets. The adjoining communities could be glimpsed also, stretching out toward the rolling hills that marked the beginning of a rural section of the state. The grass on the hillsides retained much of its color, and where the green had vanished, a golden tone had taken over that was echoed in the changing foliage.

"Well?" Ian said quietly, his hand still clasping hers.

She turned and looked at him. In the shadows of the gazebo, his blond hair seemed to be glowing, as though it had brought its own source of light with it. "Yes, it's beautiful," she sighed.

Ian's hand moved to her shoulder.

"You should try and paint it," said Lori. She felt his fingers stiffen against her and then fall away. "But you should!" she insisted.

"Hey, I agreed to drop the subject of your advice to the lovelorn of Lincoln High, so why don't you quit harping on the topic of my getting back to doing something with my talent, okay?"

"But you're wasting—"

"Hush, Lori. Be quiet and let's just look at the sunset," he said, turning toward the horizon.

"What sunset?" she said.

"Over there."

"There's no sunset over there."

"Just wait a few more seconds."

"Ian, you're crazy. There isn't going to be any sunset over there. The sky is too overcast for—"

"Hush and just watch," he said, cutting across her protests.

In one small section of the sky the grayness had broken, and from behind it there shone muted streaks of pink and gold. The sky cleared just enough for them to catch a glimpse of part of the sun itself before the shifting clouds reclaimed the horizon.

"I told you this place was magical," Ian said.

She looked up into his eyes, and slowly his face moved down toward hers. His mouth brushed her lips, kissing them lightly, and then returned for a few moments more before breaking away. She looked up at him again.

"Well?" he asked finally, not taking his eyes from hers.

"Well what?" she whispered.

"You think we have a chance?"

She didn't know how to answer him. Her eyes scanned the sky. The sun's descent was no longer visible from the gazebo, and the dark hues of evening were beginning to take over. "It's all gone," she said softly.

"No, it's not. It's still there. Just because a few clouds get in the way doesn't mean it isn't still there. If you give in to your imagination, you can light up the sky."

"And if my imagination isn't that good?"

"Here, I'll help you." He pointed to the horizon. "See right there—that streak of gold starting to break through, followed by some red, and now the orange? Can't you see that?"

He caught her chin with one hand and turned her face upward. "And maybe we'll throw in a touch of crimson, and maybe some purple, and then . . ." The rest of his words were lost in the gentle pressure of his lips against hers.

6

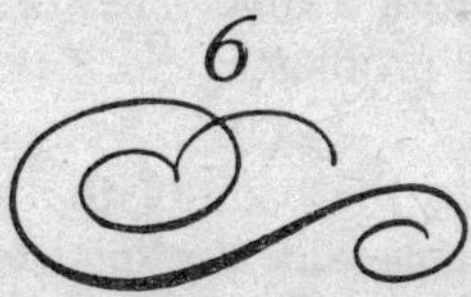

But you're all alone!" Janis said, trying to peer over Lori's shoulder. "Isn't he coming?"

"He said he might be late. His family was going up to Hampton College to see his brother play in a soccer game. He wasn't quite sure when they'd get back."

"This party's more important than a dumb soccer game." Janis moved to the side of the doorway so that Lori could enter the house. "This is the party during which everything gets solved."

"Are you sure we're going to come up with solutions for everything?" Lori asked, taking the coat hanger that Janis handed her. "I was thinking things over this afternoon, and I'm sure we're going to have huge problems just figuring out how to deal with that ugly firedoor."

79

Janis gave her a blank look.

"You know what I'm talking about, don't you?" Lori said, handing back the hanger with her jacket on it. "It's that ugly green color."

"Oh," Janis said with a laugh. "You mean all that stuff we have to deal with on the subcommittee. That can wait."

"But isn't that why we're here tonight?"

"Oh, maybe, if we have time."

"But . . ."

"Just relax and start observing. All the girls want you to observe for awhile. Then we'll start dealing with some real problems."

"Janis, I—"

"Come on to the back of the house and meet everybody," Janis said, starting to steer Lori down the hallway. "You're one of the last to get here. It's been going really well so far. My mother's being really good. She's only been popping in when the bowls of popcorn and pretzels actually do need filling. That's amazing for her."

Before they could reach the party in progress, John Kane appeared in the hallway. "Oh, there you are!" he said, his face breaking into a smile.

"Yes, here she is," Janis said. "Alone, but at least here. The next doorbell should be what's-his-name. I think I'll let you take care of that, John. Okay?"

"Sure, I'll let him in if you want me to," John said eagerly. "Should I wait by the door for awhile?"

"You're not going to wait by the door!" Janis said in her loud voice. She put her hand on his arm and began pulling him back down the hall along with Lori. "He'll arrive when he arrives. In the meantime, we're all here to have fun and to get to know each other better." She cast a knowing glance at Lori. "Let's just get in there and keep this party hopping!"

The party wasn't exactly hopping.

Most of the people in the room were gathered around the stereo system. They were looking down at the turntable, their faces heavy with concern.

"What's the matter?" Janis asked excitedly.

Everyone seemed to turn at once.

"There's something wrong with this," Laura Cooper said sadly.

"It just sort of stopped," someone else added.

"What do you mean, it just sort of stopped?" Janis said, pushing her way through to the stereo. "It was going fine when I left." She reached down and began fiddling with a series of switches.

"It started running down in the middle of a record," Laura said. "You should have heard it. I mean it made a really weird sound. And then it stopped completely. I think it's just died on us."

"It can't be dead!" Janis insisted, frantically trying to get the turntable moving once again.

Janis's mother couldn't seem to get it going either, and a group of self-appointed equipment experts among the boys had no luck in bringing it back to life despite repeated attempts. Everyone began looking at each other in disbelief.

"This is going to be *some* party," Laura could be heard muttering.

"Wait a minute, guys. What's the problem?" John Kane said. "We'll just make do with the radio." He reached for a switch on the receiver and the room was suddenly filled with loud rock 'n' roll. There was cheering and clapping and then laughter as people began pairing off. In a few seconds the place was alive with dancers.

"Thanks for coming to the rescue," Janis said to John as she adjusted the volume of the speakers so that conversation was possible.

"Anytime," John replied. "Not exactly a brilliant idea, but at least I came up with it before the crowd got too restless and decided to leave to find something better."

"There's not going to be any better party in Lincoln tonight," Janis said with annoyance. "There can't be, because we've got that all-important extra ingredient."

"Extra ingredient?"

"We've got Lori."

"Oh, yeah. Lori." John smiled at her. "I guess this *is* going to be an incredible night."

Incredible for whom? Lori was wondering an hour later.

She stared at her face in the mirror. She had taken refuge in the bathroom for a few minutes, and the face looking back at her from the glass was not that of a girl having a good time.

No sooner had the dancing begun again than girls started approaching her with their new problems. At first they did it almost surreptitiously, sidling up to her and whispering. Some had even tugged her out into the hallway so they could unburden themselves in private. But these private consultations soon became group affairs as several girls at a time began surrounding her.

They all wanted her opinions on particular boys at the party, and she was forced to make judgments based on the most superficial observations. Yet everything she said seemed to ring true to the ears of the girls listening, leading her to believe that what they really wanted was confirmation of their own intuitions.

All this time her eyes kept wandering to the front of the house in the hopes of catching a glimpse of Ian's arrival. Once he arrived the girls would give her some breathing space. Once he arrived she would become the focus of *their* observations.

But he didn't arrive, and gradually she began to doubt all that had happened between them the other night. Maybe he was staying away deliberately, suddenly afraid to face her now that the nature of their relationship had changed. They had been too caught up in a romantic daze when he had walked her home. They should have talked but they hadn't, and the next day they had been reduced to a halting conversation over the phone when their class schedules and after-school activities had kept them apart. She was beginning to wonder if perhaps the cool chill of the past few autumn mornings hadn't reminded him too much of the cold mountain daybreaks at Camp Maplewood and a time when they had shared a completely uncomplicated friendship. Maybe he didn't want to continue with what was developing now.

The door to the bathroom rattled and Janis called out, "Are you okay in there? Laura said she thought you weren't looking too well when you left."

"I'm fine," Lori answered loudly.

She quickly splashed some water on her face and patted herself dry with one of the guest towels. Perhaps Laura was right. She didn't look that well. Her short-cropped brown hair looked mousy, and the usual healthy color of her face seemed faded as she stared into the mirror above the washbasin. She didn't usually wear makeup, but she couldn't help thinking a little blusher might improve her appearance. Why was she letting the girls' demands and Ian's absence affect her so?

"Lori, are you coming out? What's-his-name has been here for five minutes. He's acting awfully shy and the girls aren't getting anywhere with him."

Lori stared at her face in the mirror again. Her hair suddenly had luster and there was color in her complexion now. Just hearing Janis speak of him, and her cheeks were flushed with an alarming redness.

"Did you hear me?" Janis asked.

"Just a minute."

Just a minute for what? To let the blood drain from her face so that it wasn't so obvious how the news of his arrival had affected her? Just a minute to let her heart recover its normal rhythm? Just a minute to dissolve the tightness that was starting to grip her throat?

Lori took a deep breath and pulled the door

open. Janis was still waiting outside, her round face creased by a frown.

"Are you sure you're okay?" the girl asked.

"Couldn't be better," Lori replied, looking over Janis's shoulder toward the room where the party was being held.

"You look a little . . . I don't know," Janis said, continuing to frown.

"I'm fine, Janis." She couldn't see anyone except John Kane, who had positioned himself in the doorway, obviously so that he could keep tabs on Janis's whereabouts. "Let's go back to the party."

"Okay," Janis said in an uncharacteristically low voice. "But promise not to crawl off into a corner with what's-his-name. I think we need you two to reenergize this whole thing. Since you've been in the bathroom, we've had several near-disasters. Some of the boys have started to congregate near the TV, and I know they're dying to plug in some of my brother's video games. We just can't let that happen."

There *was* a group of boys standing near the TV when Lori and Janis reentered the room, but none had been brave enough yet to switch on the electronic game unit. They were looking longingly at the blank screen, and a group of girls was standing behind them looking totally at a loss as to how to regain their attention. The moment Lori appeared, several of the girls began moving toward her. Lori looked for Ian, but he was nowhere in sight.

"Why don't we just tell them it's broken and then turn up the volume on the radio and demand they dance with us?" suggested Laura.

Lori found herself nodding in agreement, only half-listening. Where could Ian have gotten to?

"Well then, let's put our plan into action," Laura said. "We can't let this party get away from us."

The group of girls surrounding Lori began disbanding, retracing their route back to the boys at the TV. The moment they were gone, a girl with unruly light brown hair began to approach in a manner Lori was becoming all too used to. The girl was a complete stranger to her, yet she sensed that in a few minutes she would know more about this girl's romantic problems than she wanted to hear.

If only Ian would appear and give her an excuse to get away. If only his tall, lanky body would suddenly materialize at her side and . . . Lori felt her breath catch in her throat. Mrs. Jamison had just pushed open the kitchen door and behind her, carrying a large punchbowl, was Ian.

"It is too broken!" she heard one of the girls say with exasperation.

"No, it's not," came a boy's reply. "Look, all you have to do is push down this button and—"

And suddenly there was a fuzzy electronic buzz replacing the sound of the music coming from the stereo. In the next instant the room fell completely silent.

"Now look what you've done!" a girl near the television set gasped.

"But I didn't even *touch* the stereo system," the boy said in amazement. "All I was doing was trying to turn on the—"

Janis pushed her way through to the stereo and stared down at it. "Does anyone know anything about these things?" she asked. "I mean, the receiver's still lit up and everything."

"He must have blown the speakers," said a boy standing near the refreshment table. "Maybe you'd better check the fuses or your wiring or something."

A babble of voices rose immediately. Each person had a solution to the problem, and each solution was different. Janis seemed to be at a total loss, and for a moment her eyes settled on Lori. Lori shrugged her shoulders. This definitely wasn't her field of expertise.

"Maybe I can help," Mrs. Jamison said. "Sometimes if you just tap the left speaker and jiggle one of the knobs . . ." The guests began gathering around her as she approached the stereo.

Lori's gaze returned to Ian. His smile was already upon her, broadening as he walked across the room with the loaded punchbowl. "You thirsty?" he asked, holding it out to her.

She shook her head.

"Then let me put it down before I get frostbite."

"How've you been?" Ian asked as he set the large bowl into place in the middle of the table.

"Fine," she said, wondering if her throat was about to dry up now that she was standing so close to him. "Maybe I *could* use something to drink," she managed to get out before tightness settled into her vocal cords.

He began ladling out a cup of the reddish liquid. "Sorry I'm late," he said, lowering his voice. "We had car trouble on the way back." He placed the ladle back in the bowl and pointed at a small cut on his hand. "I'm not exactly an expert at tire changing," he said, laughing. "Or was that actually left over from the other night? Maybe it happened when I fell."

"I don't remember any cuts there," she said, accepting the glass he handed her.

"No, neither do I." His eyes sought out hers. "But then—"

His words were cut off abruptly by a loud blast from the stereo. Cheers of joy filled the room along with the music. Someone adjusted the sound only a few decibels lower, and the beat of the music continued to pulsate across the floor with deafening insistence.

Lori glanced toward the far end of the room. Mrs. Jamison was beaming. Everyone was pairing off and moving to the music as if in celebration. "Hey, you two," Janis called out. "Stop being wallflowers and show us what you can do."

Ian reached out and took Lori's glass from her hand. "Shall we?" he said, with a slight bow. "Bet you they don't realize the winners of Camp Maplewood's free-form dance competition are in attendance. Let's show them how it's really done."

He had always been a better dancer than she. She didn't have his inventiveness of movement, and she knew that it was he who made her look good. His new height had added no trace of the awkwardness tall people sometimes revealed on the dance floor. If anything, he was even more graceful than she remembered. His lanky frame moved to the music as if the beat came from somewhere inside his body, and his golden curls hit against the side of his neck with unrestrained abandon.

Some of the other couples stopped dancing and began moving to the sides of the room to watch. Lori knew that she and Ian were gradually becoming the focus of everyone's attention, yet somehow she didn't mind. It felt good to be caught up in the music, to be moving in time with him.

The song was drawing to a close and Ian began moving in closer. On the very last note, he leaned down and briefly kissed her.

His hand reached out to hers as the next number began, but before he could draw her into its slower rhythms, Janis's voice cut between them. "Boy, that was really something," she said. "There won't be any point in even having a contest during the next dance at school. You two will win hands down."

"She's right," chimed in John. "I don't even think I'm going to show up at that dance if you two are going to be there."

"Oh, don't worry," Janis said. "We'll make them dance in the coat room so that the rest of us don't have to mope around all evening with inferiority complexes."

"Where'd you learn to dance so well?" John asked Ian. "Did you take lessons?"

Ian shook his head. "I've just always danced. Even when I was a little kid I always danced."

Lori turned to John. "When we were at camp, all the older boys used to get really annoyed with him because the older girls always wanted him as a partner."

"I think the younger girls in this room wouldn't mind. . . . Well, anyway," Janis laughed. She turned her large brown eyes up to Ian's face. "So I hear you and Lori have been an item for years and years and years."

"An item?" Ian said.

"Since way back at that camp."

"Janis . . ." Lori felt like sinking into the floor.

"Well, didn't you tell me . . . ?" She turned to John. "I mean, are they the perfect couple, or aren't they?"

John seemed embarrassed by her question.

Janis looked up at Ian once again. "You're probably the person who's responsible for all our good luck," she said.

"Good luck?"

"Lori probably learned all about love from you," Janis said brightly.

Lori didn't dare look at Ian.

Janis poked her finger lightly against Ian's shirt. "Maybe you could start giving some advice to the guys around here. I mean, I'm sure John here wouldn't mind picking up some pointers from—"

"You want to dance, Janis?" John interrupted, boldly grabbing at her hand.

Janis pulled free. "Now see," she said, "that's no way to ask someone to dance. I'm sure Ian would never do it that way. Show him how you'd ask Lori to dance."

Ian's face looked frozen.

"You don't have to be so shy around us," Janis laughed. "Just give John a few pointers on—"

"I don't need any pointers," John said, once again tugging at her arm. "Let's dance. I like this song."

Janis groaned. "Just give him a few words of advice," she begged Ian. "Life would be so much easier at Lincoln High if the guys would only—"

"He doesn't need me to give him any advice," Ian said sharply.

"Well, if he doesn't have you, then who can he turn to?" Janis said with mild exasperation.

"Let's just dance," John said, his hand gripping her arm tightly. "If I need advice, I can always find it."

"Oh, yeah? Where?"

"Around."

"Around where?"

"Well, I've already gotten some from the same source you use," he said angrily.

Janis' eyes darted toward Lori. "You're kidding," she said. "You mean you consulted . . . ? You know, I sort of wondered if that might happen. Maybe the guys at Lincoln aren't as slow as I thought they were."

"John's the only one who—"

"Oh, don't worry, Lori. None of the girls is going to get upset if you help out the boys a little."

"You bet! We're willing to share you," a girl said from behind Lori. "But right now, . . . well, could you just step over here for a few minutes? You see that guy in the white shirt, the one standing next to the stereo pretending not to notice me? Maybe if we found a quiet corner, you could tell me—"

"Office hours are closed for today," Ian said brusquely. His hand reached for Lori's and he began steering her toward the refreshment table.

"But I only wanted her to—"

"I already told you, office hours are closed!" Ian snapped back at the girl.

Lori was glad to escape, but she wasn't too happy with the way Ian's fingers were digging into her arm. By the time he got her to the punchbowl she was starting to feel real pain.

"Ian, let go," she said. "You're holding me too tightly."

He gave her an odd look, but his hand didn't fall away.

"Ian . . . you're hurting me." She felt a current of anger run through her. "You didn't have to lead me away with such force," she complained.

"Well, someone had to before you let that girl just barge in and begin to ruin everything."

"She wasn't going to ruin everything!"

"No, she was just going to drag you into a corner and force you back into your role as Advice Goddess of Lincoln High."

"She wasn't going to force me into doing anything," Lori said, glaring up into Ian's face.

"Yes," he said, shaking his head sadly. "I guess you're right. She wasn't going to force you at all. You would have gladly fallen back into that idiotic role without any pressure. You love playing that part, don't you?"

"Maybe I'm good at it," Lori said. "I can't just turn my back on my friends if they want me to help them with their problems. They need me," she added more firmly.

"Need what?" he asked angrily. "You're no more experienced than they are! How come you're pretending to have all this wisdom?"

"How do you know what's happened to me in the past couple of years? Some of us have been growing up, you know," she retorted.

Ian didn't respond, but the muscles in his face became taut and his eyes turned icy.

"Hey, you guys," Janis's voice said from behind them. "Stop hogging all the food and come back and join the party. We need you two to show us how to dance."

"I'm really not hungry," Lori said brusquely. "And I don't feel like dancing right now."

Janis stared at her in amazement. "Okay, it was just a suggestion," she said. "But why don't you join the rest of us? We do have to sort of talk about decorating that dumb entranceway. I mean, that *is* the point of this party, isn't it?" She laughed. "Or is that what you two were talking about over here anyway? You've probably got the whole thing planned and there's nothing more to work out."

"Oh, there's lots to work out," Lori said, glancing quickly at Ian. "Lots and lots to work out."

His face hadn't lost its coldness. "Yes," he concurred. "In fact there might be too much to work out."

"Too much?" Janis laughed. "Stop worrying. We'll get things straightened out. With Lori's talents we're bound to come up with something really exciting. We'll end up impressing the whole school!"

"I'd say Lori's talents have already impressed the whole school," Ian said with a curious smile. "It's only the immature and unsophisticated ones amongst us who don't seem to appreciate them."

"Huh?" Janis said with nervous laughter. "What's he talking about? What immature and unsophisticated ones?"

Lori avoided Ian's gaze. She stared out beyond Janis's shoulders at the dancers near the stereo.

"Are you two okay?" Janis asked, her smile disappearing.

"Oh, we're in tip-top shape," Ian said. "Come on, Lori. Let's get out on that floor and let them see what tip-top shape we're in." He held his hand out to her. "Come on, let's put on a great show!"

Lori didn't want to dance with him at the moment. She wanted to flee back to the bathroom and splash water on her face and let the anger that was racing through her slowly die away.

"Are you just going to stand there?" Janis said. "There are lots of girls at this party who'd be thrilled to death just to get a chance to dance with Ian, and you're just going to stand there? I mean, I'd just love to . . ." She swallowed the end of her sentence as she realized what she was about to say.

"Then why don't you?" Lori replied coolly.

"Sure, why don't you," Ian said, his curious smile returning. "Since Lori obviously doesn't want to join me, why don't you give me a break?"

"Oh, no. I didn't mean . . . I'm really not much of a dancer," Janis said nervously.

"Come on, Janis," Ian insisted, his smile growing wider. "Lori looks like she wants to sit this one out, so let's get out there before the song's over."

"But I can't dance with someone else's . . . I mean . . ." Her eyes turned to Lori. "Would you mind?" she asked almost breathlessly.

Lori couldn't help laughing. "No, go ahead," she said.

"Well then, maybe you can dance with John." Janis looked around the room quickly. "If you can find him," she said.

"Come on, Janis," Ian said, extending his hand. "Let's dance."

Lori watched as he led her friend out onto the floor. Janis seemed to freeze at first when Ian began moving in time to the beat, but in a few seconds she was trying rather wildly to match all of his steps.

Lori retreated to the side wall and leaned against it, closing her eyes. The evening could only get worse, she decided. It hurt to see him moving so gracefully out there, even if it was only with Janis.

"She's not that good, is she?" a pained voice said next to her.

Lori's eyes flashed open to discover John Kane standing by her side.

"Of course, she's a great girl and all that," he continued. "But as a dancer she's . . . well, I guess I shouldn't be talking. Compared to Ian, I'm not that hot either. How come he's so good at it? You think maybe if I was more athletic or more sophisticated I might . . ." John's face broke into a smile. "I guess I'm never going to be either of those things, am I?" he said. "And I guess I shouldn't be bothering you with my problems anymore, should I? I get the impression Ian thinks we've been dumping too much into your lap, so I guess I'll just have to start keeping things to myself again."

"Don't pay any attention to him," Lori said with a hint of bitterness. "I don't mind people coming to me with their problems if I can really help them."

John looked relieved. "You helped me a lot. This party was a much better way of getting to know Janis than some kind of nervous date where . . . well, you understand." He stared out at the dance floor and his smile disappeared.

Lori looked into his face. "You want to dance?" she asked.

He seemed startled. "Oh, I don't know if that would be such a good idea," he said.

"Why not?"

A tentative smile formed on his lips. "Do you think she'd mind?" he asked.

"No, it'll be okay with her."

His smile vanished. "It will?"

"Sure."

"You mean she won't even be a little bit jealous?" He sounded disappointed.

"Who knows?" Lori laughed. "Maybe it's something you should risk."

"Is that the advice you're giving me?" John asked seriously.

"Yes," she said. "That's the advice I'm giving you."

"Well then . . ." He still hesitated. "Are you sure?"

Lori nodded. "Yes," she said, glaring at Ian. "Take my word for it."

"Okay," John said eagerly. "Then let's get out there and show them what we can do!"

"Neither of them are that great dancers, are they?" Ian said, reaching up for a low-hanging branch and pulling off some of the leaves.

Lori didn't look over at him. "At least they're enthusiastic," she replied, her voice still governed by a tightness that didn't seem to want to leave.

"Yes, especially Janis." His laughter sounded forced. He had insisted on walking her home when she had announced her early departure, despite the fact that they had had little to do with each other over the past hour or so. They walked silently along the dark streets.

"They were enjoying themselves, though," Ian said, letting the leaves fall to the ground.

"Why shouldn't they have been?"

"Well they were dancing with us, for one thing." His laughter sounded unnatural. "You can't say we were exactly in the greatest of moods."

"I didn't mind dancing with John," she said, staring down at the sidewalk.

"That's not what I meant. We weren't in a bad mood because of them. We were in a bad mood because of each other and what we said."

She felt herself bristling. "It seems to me you were the one doing most of the talking."

He came to a complete stop. "Would you please just look at me?" he requested. She came to a reluctant halt and glanced at his face. "I'm sorry if

I came on so strong, but I just had to say what was on my mind. Maybe you're right. Maybe I haven't grown up as much as you in the past few years, but I still don't see why you find this role of advice giver so . . . so . . ." He gave up searching for the right word. "Oh, what does it matter? I don't want everything ruined between us because of what happened tonight." His hand came out to her shoulder and squeezed it. "I still want to be your friend, Lori."

She had been slowly warming to his apology, but the minute he uttered the word friend, she felt the return of her earlier resentment. She didn't want to look into his face any longer. She wanted to be home and away from him.

"What's wrong?" he asked. "I promise I won't ever act like that again if that's what you're worried about."

"Can't you at least give me a smile?" he asked. "So don't forgive me right away, but at least grant me a smile."

"Ian, I'm tired."

"Oh, come on, Lori. Just curl your lips a little bit and assure me that things will be all right between us. You can't just throw away everything that exists because of one little fight, can you? Give a guy a break."

She sighed and then managed an approximation of a smile.

He looked disappointed. "Can't you do better than that?"

"Ian . . ."

They were at the turnoff to her block. "You

don't need to walk me any further," she said. "I can get home safely from here."

"What would your mom think if I didn't deliver you right to your doorstep?" he said, turning the corner with her.

"It wasn't exactly a date," she reminded him. "You didn't pick me up and take me to the party."

"Well, I would have if I hadn't had to go on that family outing," he said and then paused. "What do you mean, it wasn't a date?"

"It wasn't," she insisted.

He fell silent for a few seconds as they approached the walkway leading up to her house. "So in your book you don't count this as a date," he said. "I guess I must seem awfully unsophisticated to you for calling it one." His voice was cold. "Well, that's okay, I guess. Maybe in the future I should be coming to you for advice about such things."

"Don't be silly. I only meant—"

"I'm not being silly. I'm being perfectly serious. If what all the others are saying is true, I could probably learn a lot from you."

His words weren't making any sense to her. A dull ache was beginning to grow in her head, and she was happy at the sight of the comforting light in the front window and the haven of the bedroom awaiting her upstairs.

He didn't say anything more, but he kept walking with her right up to the front door.

"So I'll be seeing you tomorrow," he said. "I'll even try to arrive with some ideas."

She looked at him blankly.

"That meeting Janis said we had to have because we got nothing done tonight. The one she wants to have in Webster Park," he said, laughing.

Lori felt a real smile come to her lips.

"That's better," Ian said. "Now go get some sleep."

He bent his head. She pulled back in confusion and his kiss landed awkwardly at the side of her mouth. When he stretched up to his full height once again, he stared into her eyes and then broke out into a smile that didn't conceal his own confusion.

"Guess I do need some advice," he murmured. His hand grazed her shoulder, but he managed to give her the usual squeeze. "See you tomorrow," he said.

She watched him walk slowly to the sidewalk. He hesitated as he reached the street and then turned. There was no parting wave. She watched him as he stepped from the curb and suddenly took off in a run.

7

What are all those papers?" Amanda asked. She stood in the doorway of Lori's room, her hand turning the knob back and forth with great vigor.

"Sketches," Lori said.

"You've sure done a lot of them."

Lori stared down at the drawings surrounding her. "It's not so many."

"They cover the whole bed."

"Some of them are just rough ideas."

"Of what?"

Lori looked up. "Stop playing with the doorknob," she said. "You might break it."

Amanda gave her sister a look of exasperation. "The doorknob's not going to break. It's strong. Stronger than I am, in fact, which is pretty amazing, if you ask me."

"I'm not asking you."

"Well, who cares anyway."

"Amanda, I don't need this kind of dumb conversation right now. I have to get these ready for this afternoon's meeting."

Amanda gave the doorknob one last rough twist and moved into the room. "What's that supposed to be?" she said, pointing at a sketch at the foot of the bed. "It looks like a pile of leaves."

"That's just what it is."

"I don't get it. How come you're drawing piles of leaves when you're supposed to be planning decorations?"

"The leaves are part of the decorations."

"Huh?"

"It's the fall dance, so I thought we could scatter leaves along the entranceway and then have them piled high around the door."

Amanda stared down at the sketches in disbelief. "You really think you're going to get away with that?" she said, shaking her head from side to side.

"*Leaves?*" Janis said incredulously into the telephone. "You really think Mrs. Rinehart will let us scatter leaves all along the floor and then . . . ? I don't know, Lori. I think she might not be too crazy about bringing real leaves inside."

"Well, it's just an idea," Lori said, trying to hide her disappointment at Janis's reaction. "Maybe someone else will come up with something better at the meeting."

"Yeah, maybe."

"We *are* still having that meeting this afternoon, aren't we?"

"Meeting?"

"In the park."

"Oh. Is that going to be a meeting? I thought we were just having an outing to help smooth things over. Or have you already done that?"

"Done what?"

"Smoothed things over with what's-his-name. I think maybe it was a bad idea for me to have danced with him so much last night. I got the impression that you and John didn't exactly appreciate it."

"Janis, what are you talking about?"

"Well, I know John and you were both trying to put a good face on things by dancing with each other, but I could sort of tell that—"

"John and I had fun dancing together," Lori interrupted.

"You did?" There was silence for a few seconds. "You mean he was enjoying himself?"

"I think so."

"He wasn't even a tiny bit upset that I was dancing with someone as tall as what's-his-name? Not even a tiny bit upset?"

"Why? Was he supposed to get upset?"

"Well, I figured it might be a way of testing his reactions to some competition. Not that what's-his-name is really competition. I mean, everyone knows that he's yours, and that you two were just sort of having fun pretending you weren't getting along so that when you got back together it would be even better than before. Or am I reading things all wrong? You two just seem to have such a sophisticated relationship." There was another pause. "So you-know-who really enjoyed dancing with you?" she said finally.

"Can we get back to the topic of the meeting?" Lori said impatiently. "Are we all just going to meet there, or what?"

"Oh, I guess you two had already left before we set up anything definite. We're all going to show up at the main gate at two o'clock and then spend the afternoon on the lake. We can rent boats, so bring some money."

"But we *are* going to have a meeting, aren't we?"

"I guess so. We can yell from boat to boat or something."

"Janis . . ."

"We'll have the meeting afterwards," Janis assured her. "Gosh, Lori, sometimes you get so serious about things."

"Well, if you haven't forgotten, I *am* the head of this subcommittee."

"Don't worry. The entranceway will be a knockout, even if it is just brown leaves."

"Not brown leaves. Colorful ones. Yellows and oranges and maybe lit from underneath so that the piles seem to be glowing."

Janis laughed. "Mrs. Rinehart is going to have a fit!" she said. "But it sounds better and better to me the more you describe it. What does what's-his-name think of it?"

"I don't know. I haven't discussed it with him," Lori admitted.

Janis laughed again. "I guess you two had more important things to discuss."

"What's that supposed to mean?"

"Stop taking me so seriously! Everything I say doesn't have to have a meaning. Things just pop out of my mouth." Janis's laughter stopped. "Which is probably why I'll never have the kind of relationships that you do," she said with a tinge of regret. "But then, I'm me and you're you and at least I've got you as a friend to steer me back on course when I start—"

"Janis, I'll see you at two."

"Don't forget to bring what's-his-name," Janis said rapidly. "I can't wait to see those long arms rowing you across the lake. I mean, talk about romantic images!"

"Sounds great to me," Ian said. "In fact it's a lot better than anything I've come up with."

She had agreed to meet him at the park gate, hoping the rest of the kids would already be there. But no one was on time, and she was alone with him again. The skies were growing cloudy and there was a chill in the air. They stood next to the brick wall, and she told him about her ideas for decorating the gym entranceway.

She had left the sketches at home, convinced that nothing was going to be decided on the outing, but now she was explaining everything to Ian. She tried not to notice the way his curls were blowing in the breeze or the way his finger kept running along the lines of mortar between the rows of bricks. She concentrated on the plans for the dance, relieved that they had such a subject to discuss.

"What have you come up with?" she asked,

looking beyond him, hoping to catch a glimpse of the arrival of the others.

"Oh, I don't know," he said. "Since the theme is the autumn harvest I was thinking in terms of pumpkins and dried corn and things like that. Have they come to any decision about what the inside of the gym is going to look like?"

Lori smiled. "Pumpkins and dried corn, I think," she said. "And the refreshment stand in the form of a half-built barn. And lots of dark blue sky and stars and a harvest moon."

"Original stuff, I see."

"What else are we supposed to do with a theme like that? I wouldn't be surprised if Mrs. Rinehart threw out the rock band and insisted on square dance music."

"She'd never get away with it."

"No, probably not."

"Do you think she'll really let you bring bushels of leaves into the entranceway?"

Lori shrugged. "I guess we could make them out of construction paper and tape them to the floor, but it wouldn't be the same. I wanted to go for something a little more . . . I don't know . . . a little more mysterious, I guess. Like a walk through the autumn woods in the moonlight."

"Sounds good to me." Their eyes met for a moment and then both of them looked away. "Lori," he said, flicking off some loose mortar from between the bricks. "I was thinking about last night and—"

"Hey, you two!" Janis's voice cut between them sharply. "Let's get this afternoon underway before raindrops start falling on our heads." John Kane was trailing behind her, and behind him were several other couples, none of whom were members of Lori's committee. "Come on, the boats are this way," Janis yelled, not bothering to stop as she passed by.

"Looks like she wants us to move." Ian laughed.

"So has everybody got their watches synchronized?" John said. "We've all paid for a full hour, which means we have to be back by three twenty-two exactly."

"Three-thirty," Janis said, climbing into one of the boats. "They don't time you that strictly."

"Okay then, three-thirty. Or thereabouts," he added, shaking his wrist and then turning to Janis. "Am I with you?" he asked.

"I don't know. Are you?" she asked, rolling her eyeballs upwards at Lori.

"I'm a pretty good rower, you know," he said.

"Then prove it."

The other couples began pushing off from the dock. Neither Lori nor Ian had claimed a boat yet, and soon they were the only ones not out on the water.

"Well?" Ian said finally. "Which one looks most seaworthy to you?"

Lori scanned the row of boats. "None of them looks too sturdy to me."

"I know what you mean," Ian said and laughed. "I don't think they're going to skim along the water like the canoes at . . . well, at least they won't be capsizing either."

"Unless we get caught in a rough storm," Lori said, nodding toward the darkening sky.

"Well, there's definitely not going to be a glorious sunset tonight." His face suddenly froze as he realized what he had said. "I mean, it doesn't exactly look that way," he added awkwardly. "How about this one?" he said. "I'll row for a while and you can steer me and then maybe we'll change places. That okay with you?"

The boat moved more gracefully than either of them had expected. It didn't have the swiftness of the canoes at camp, but the steady pull of Ian's strong arms sent it out rapidly toward the center of the lake.

"Should we try and catch up to the others?" he asked.

"Janis said we're supposed to have our meeting by yelling from boat to boat."

Ian laughed and stopped rowing. He glanced toward the cluster of boats near the far shore. "We don't really want to join them, do we?" he asked. "Let's find out where that inlet leads."

It led to an entirely different section of the lake, but Ian didn't seem satisfied until he had crossed it and moved into a narrow arm of water whose banks were overgrown with low-hanging trees.

"You think this goes anywhere?" he asked.

Lori glanced down at her watch. "You want me to take over the rowing?"

"No. Let's just let the boat drift for awhile." He pulled the oars into the boat. "Maybe the flow of the water will take us someplace interesting."

The sluggish flow of the water moved the boat

under a tree against the bank where its prow got caught between two large roots growing out from the lakeside.

"Here, give me the oar and I'll get us loose," Lori said.

"Why don't we just stay here?" Ian stretched out his long legs and extended his arms to the oarlocks. "We could talk for a while," he suggested, staring up at the tree branch above them. "I think I need to consult with you."

"Consult with me?"

"I've been thinking a lot about what happened between us last night and I've come to the conclusion that I could probably learn a lot from you."

Lori glanced at the bank of the river. Suddenly she was feeling very uncomfortable about being trapped in that boat with him.

"I have this friend, you see. He needs your help a lot."

"A friend?"

"Yes, a friend," he laughed. "A tall, skinny guy with blond hair whose mother always thinks it needs cutting. You get the picture?"

Lori nodded. "I think I've seen him in the halls of Lincoln High," she said. "In fact, I think he's on my subcommittee."

"Yes, that's the guy," Ian said, running his fingers along the bark of the branch as he reached upwards. "Just an overgrown kid if you ask me, but I've known him a long time and I don't want to turn my back on him, so I told him I'd ask a real expert about his dilemma." He paused a moment. "You see, there's this girl."

Lori glanced upward at some of the branches. "Now, he'd like to—"

"Do you think that limb would hold me?" she asked, pointing to the thickest one she could find.

Ian looked at her in astonishment. "I didn't know you were still interested in such things," he said.

"It's better than just sitting here and—"

"And listening to my friend's problems?"

"And waiting for the rain," she said with a glare.

"Maybe you're right." He looked at the branch. "You want a leg up?" he asked, starting to get to his feet.

"I think I'll just pull myself up," she said. "It's low enough."

She began getting to her feet too, and the boat shifted against the roots.

"Whoa!" he cautioned, holding his hands out to her shoulders to steady her.

"I'm not going to fall," she said, shaking free of his grip.

"You're pretty sure of yourself this afternoon, aren't you?"

"Why shouldn't I be?" she snapped back, reaching for the branch.

"Ah, the voice of experience speaking," he said. "Okay, let's see you climb that tree."

It wasn't an easy thing to accomplish. The dexterity she had once possessed didn't come back readily. It was a struggle to lift herself up and a struggle to position herself on the branch, but once she was above the boat she felt a curious exhilaration as she looked down at the top of Ian's head.

"Aren't you going any higher than that?" He laughed. "You never used to stop 'til you reached the very top."

"I like it where I am."

"Do you want me to join you?"

She jiggled the branch with her feet. "I don't know if it's strong enough to hold both of us."

"Should we risk it?"

He didn't wait for her response. She watched with envy the ease with which his arms lifted him upward and then noted smugly how he, too, had to struggle somewhat to get his legs over the branch. He had been a lot more adept at tree climbing years ago.

"So," he said, drawing himself up, not quite able to stand at his full height because of the crisscross of branches above. "Now that we're here, can we continue our consultation?"

She felt a sense of panic overtake her. "I think I *will* try for the top," she murmured, moving out farther on the limb and stretching toward a nearby branch.

"Hey!" Ian warned. "You're going out too far!"

"No, I'm not."

"It's not going to support both of us if you move out—"

There was the sound of cracking. She remembered reaching out for a branch and suddenly the branch was no longer there. The next thing she knew she was falling through the air and then plunging into the water. She came up spluttering, her arm hitting the wooden side of the boat. As she tried to grab it, the water splashed behind her and

Ian came to the surface. His wet curls were clinging to the sides of his face and he was actually smiling.

"I told you not to go out any farther," he remonstrated laughingly as she began awkwardly trying to get back into the boat. The added weight of her wet clothes seemed to make the task impossible. "What's your hurry?" he asked. "Now that we're drenched, we might as well enjoy the water."

"Oh, grow up!" she said, the anger in her body giving her the extra strength finally to pull herself over the side of the vessel. "We could have been killed if we'd hit the boat instead of the water!"

"So let's celebrate our survival by taking a swim."

"It's freezing in there."

"It'll be warmer here than where you are once the wind gets to you."

"Oh, shut up, Ian! Go take your swim and I'll meet you back at the dock." Shivering, she reached for the oars.

"Hey! You can't leave me here!"

"Why not? I think you'd really enjoy the long swim back to the boat-rental place."

"Oh, be nice, Lori. If you row away now, we won't be able to finish that consultation in private. My friend really needs your help."

"Go tell your friend to go jump in the lake!" she said, jamming the oars into their locks. "You two can have lots of fun having a great swim together!"

"But what about that girl?"

"That girl's going back to shore to get warm."

Ian's face appeared over the side of the boat. "I

didn't know she was here today," he said, without smiling.

Lori glanced at him with annoyance.

"I thought she was somewhere else. Most likely upstate at his brother's college where he met her yesterday," Ian said coolly. "There are lots of sophisticated girls up there. Lots and lots of them. And it only took a moment for my friend to . . . well, you know how it is . . ."

Lori pushed at the roots of the tree and began dislodging the boat. There was no reason to stay there and listen to all this nonsense while the shivers up her back were increasing.

Ian continued to hold on to the boat as it pushed off from shore. "Of course, my friend's just an overgrown kid without much experience, and he was wondering—"

"You know, you're getting to be a real drag on this boat," she said. "I could make a lot faster time if you'd either climb on board or let go completely."

"Maybe I will just swim back to the dock," he said.

"Suit yourself."

"It might give me some time to think about my friend and what the future holds for him. This girl is really something else and he doesn't quite know what to do next. You got any suggestions I could mull over while I make my way back to shore?"

"Consulting hours are over for today!" she said with undisguised fury.

"Oh, I see. Well, maybe tomorrow then."

She cast him the coldest look imaginable and whipped the oars around, almost hitting him with one of the blades as it came out of the water.

"Guess you want me to let go, don't you," he said, still not laughing.

"It would help a lot if you did."

"Well, then, maybe I will for the time being."

He released his hold on the side of the boat and his face disappeared from sight. She watched it reappear seconds later at the stern before she began rowing once again.

She felt anger and guilt and confusion as she recrossed the various parts of the lake. She shouldn't have left him out there, despite the fact that she knew he was an excellent swimmer. As she approached the dock, she became aware that the first drops of rain were starting to spatter against the interior of the boat. She looked back and couldn't see Ian, and then suddenly she was being greeted with consternation by her fellow students.

"What happened?" Janis called out before she even pulled in to the wooden structure. "Where's Ian?"

"He's coming," Lori said, sensing that the shivers were about to overtake her even more now that she had reached the shore. "We had an accident."

"An accident!"

"Not with the boat. We were in a tree—"

Janis wasn't listening. "But where is he? Where's Ian?"

"He's coming," Lori repeated. She turned as she stepped onto the dock and looked back across the water. There was no one in sight. Another shiver traveled up her back, a shiver that had nothing to do with her wet clothes or the chilly wind or the rain. "He's swimming back," she said feebly.

"Swimming!"

"He wanted to," Lori insisted, her voice beginning to quiver. "He's really a good swimmer. This distance would be nothing to him."

"But it's starting to rain," Janis said, raising her hand to shield her eyes as she looked out into the grayness. "He might not be able to see where he's—"

"What seems to be the problem here?" a man's voice asked. Lori swung around to discover the boat-rental agent coming towards her. "What did we have here, a capsize?" he said, glancing at the state of Lori's clothes.

She tried to explain what had happened, but her voice was shaking. "And he said he was swimming back?" he asked. "In all his clothes and in this kind of weather?" Lori found herself gulping as she nodded. The rain was beginning to come down in earnest now, hitting her head and shoulders with punishing intensity.

"We're going to have to send someone out there," the man said, yelling back to his assistant. He turned to Lori. "You'd better come with us so that we can see just exactly where you left him."

The man moved down the dock a few yards and began untying a motorboat from one of the moorings.

"Don't worry, Lori. They'll find him," John said, coming to her side. "Ian shouldn't have any trouble out in that water if he's the swimmer you say he is."

"That's right," Janis added. "Ian's really strong."

Lori stared out into the blowing rain. "I shouldn't have left him there," she murmured. "I should have known better."

"I thought you said he *wanted* to swim back," John said.

"He did," Lori sighed, "but I should have insisted that he get back in the boat. I was just so angry at him and I . . ."

"Stop blaming yourself," said Janis. She turned to John. "Why don't you go and try to find Lori a blanket? She looks like she's getting awfully cold."

John headed toward the boat-rental office, leaving Lori and Janis alone at the end of the dock.

"What if something has happened to him?" Lori said, no longer trying to fight back the tears.

"He'll be all right," said Janis, bringing her arm up to her friend's shoulder and giving her a hug.

"But I'll feel so guilty if something *has* happened."

"There's no need for that," a voice said from behind them.

"Ian!" Lori gasped, turning to the drenched figure standing only a few feet away. "How did you get here?" she asked.

"Walked," he said simply.

"Walked?"

"When it started raining I decided I'd better not risk getting caught in the middle of the lake with no visibility, so I swam to shore, and now here I am. Wet and cold," he laughed, "but nothing for you to feel guilty about."

"But we thought you might have . . . well, you know," Janis said.

"Didn't Lori tell you I know how to swim?"

"Yes, she told us, but it still gave us all a scare when you didn't show up behind her. There's a man getting ready right this minute to take out a motorboat and start looking for you." Janis glanced back down the dock. "I guess someone should tell him it won't be necessary now."

"Yes," Ian said, pushing back the curls of hair clinging to the sides of his neck. "Why don't you go and tell him, so that we can all get out of here quickly and find someplace warm and sheltered."

"I'll only be a second," said Janis. "Don't disappear on us again, okay?"

"I'll stay right where I am."

"I'll see if John has found some blankets."

"Good idea."

He waited until Janis was several yards away before speaking again. "You were worried, huh?" he asked.

"Yes, I was worried," she admitted.

"Did you really think I had drowned?"

"I didn't know what to think."

A smile flashed across his lips. "I wouldn't go and drown on you, Lori," he said. "I'm just not that kind of guy."

"But you did enjoy throwing a good scare into me," she said angrily.

"I didn't do it deliberately."

"Oh, no? It sounds like just the kind of thing a little boy would think was a really great trick."

"It wasn't a trick," he said, the anger in his voice

matching hers now. "You'd know that if you could clear your mind of all the clutter that's taken over lately and see things for what they really are. You're so caught up in a world of schemes and plots and maneuverings that you can't begin to—"

"Oh, I can see perfectly well, Ian Winslow," she said coldly. "Don't tell me my vision is growing cloudy just because you don't like the reflection of yourself you're seeing in my eyes."

"What's that supposed to mean?"

"It seems obvious to me. Maybe your friend could explain it to you. Or maybe that college girl he knows could explain it to him and then pass the word on to you."

"Maybe she just can."

The rain was turning into a fine drizzle, misting the air with moisture that blurred images just a few feet away. Lori hugged herself tightly in a vain attempt to stop her teeth from chattering. She didn't notice the arm stretching toward her until it was already at her back. It pulled her to him, and for a moment, as she sensed the warmth beneath his soaked exterior, her shivers disappeared.

But her mind was too aware of the fact that the arm holding her, the arm attempting to offer her a comforting haven against his chest belonged to Ian Winslow, and a part of her rebelled. She pushed away, saying, "Don't," and once again curled her arms around herself.

"Why not?" he said.

She looked up into the blur of his face. "You're all wet," she murmured.

"*I'm* all wet!" His words came out in a strangled

tone, caught somewhere between laughter and anger.

Lori couldn't stare into his face any longer. It was expressing too much of the pain and confusion she herself was experiencing. She turned almost desperately as shivers continued to travel up her back. At that moment, Janis appeared with blankets.

8

"**B**ut I can't miss another day of school. I'm going to be so far behind I'll never catch up," Lori said, propping herself on her elbows.

"You're still not in any shape to go back to classes." Mrs. Kennedy gestured to Lori to sit back against the pillows so that the breakfast tray could be put in place. "The doctor says you should have a few more days of rest."

"But what about the decorating committee?"

"I thought your friend Janis told me everything was running smoothly, that everyone was putting your plans into action and all the materials would be ready when you returned to school."

"But how do I know they're doing it right?" Lori asked, looking down at the tray. How many times was she going to be served poached eggs this week?

"You can trust them, can't you?"

"But I never did get to explain all the details." Lori looked at her mother reproachfully. "And now that you've cut off all incoming calls to me . . ."

"Honey, they're still coming every half hour at night, and I'm not going to have any daughter of mine half killing herself trying to answer them. I explain very patiently to everyone who phones that—"

"But they need me," Lori sighed.

"They can fend for themselves for awhile," said Mrs. Kennedy. "Now try to eat all of your breakfast for a change. We need to build up your strength so that you can get back on your feet."

"I can get back on my feet right now," Lori said, digging her fork into the yellow of the egg and watching it begin to spread across the piece of toast.

"I'm sure you can, baby." Mrs. Kennedy laughed. "But I just want to be sure you're completely better. In a few more years you'll be out on your own and you can half kill yourself if you want to, but at the moment you're my sick little girl and I'm going to nurse you back to health if it kills me."

"Are you still sick?" Amanda asked with disgust.

"According to Mom I am."

"You want some company?"

"Sure, come on in. Tell me what life is like in the outside world." Lori pushed some magazines aside and made room on the bed for her sister. "Of course, I'm assuming the outside world is still there."

"It's there," said Amanda. "It's been asking about you, too."

"Mom won't let me take any phone calls."

"I mean it's been asking about you in person."

"So?" Lori said, feigning disinterest.

"You want your message?"

"What message?"

"This one," Amanda said, twisting so that she could reach into the back pocket of her jeans. She pulled out a folded envelope. "I'll give you three guesses who it's from."

"Amanda . . . !"

"You have to guess first."

"Why do I have to do that?"

"Because I say so. Besides, it's a lot more fun this way. Go ahead and take a guess. I'll give you a hint. It's from a guy."

"Robert Redford," Lori said.

"Be serious."

"Okay. John Travolta. I hear he's in town and just dying to see me."

"No, a guy you know. Someone you go to school with. But just remember, it's your third guess."

Lori sighed. "Let's see," she said, closing her eyes and frowning in mock concentration. "No, it couldn't be him. He doesn't know I exist. And that other guy is much too shy. I guess it just has to be . . . no, probably not him either. I don't think he's the note-writing type. I guess there really is only one person it could be."

"Well, who do you think?" Amanda asked with exasperation.

"Oh, I guess it's that tall blond kid. You know—Ian what's-his-name."

"Winslow," Amanda said with disappointment.

"So hand it over and let me read it."

"Not until you take your extra guess."

"But I already got it right."

"You did?"

"I said it's from Ian."

"It's not from him."

"It isn't?"

"No, it's from some short little stocky kid who says he's that Janis's boyfriend. He says you'll know who he is."

"It's from John Kane?"

"Yeah, I think that's his name. He was waiting for me out on the sidewalk, and the minute I started up toward the door he called me back." Amanda patted her front pocket. "He pays well."

"You took money from him!"

"He forced me to."

"I'll bet."

Amanda held out the envelope. "You don't seem too eager to read it," she said. "If it had been from Ian, I know you'd be grabbing it from me really fast."

"Ian's just a friend."

The eleven-year-old rolled her eyeballs upward.

"Well he *is*, Amanda."

"I heard you the first time." Amanda pushed the envelope onto her sister's lap. "I think I'll leave you alone to read this in peace. If you want to send a message back to that little guy, I'll give you a bargain rate, seeing as how you're my sister and sick in bed and everything."

"Amanda . . . I don't think—" but Amanda had already left.

Lori waited until her sister was in the hall before she began opening the envelope. The message inside was on two sheets of paper.

"Dear Lori," the top sheet of paper read. "I hope you're starting to feel better. Your mother won't let any of us talk to you for a few days until you get your strength back, which I hope is soon. Janis hopes that your mother will let her visit you if she begs a lot and stretches the truth a bit about how the decorating plans are going. Actually, things are going fine according to Janis, but she's sorry that she let your mother know that, because now she's going to have to fib some to get in to see you in person."

Lori's eyes began skimming the bottom half of the page. It was filled with the same rambling, repetitive sentences, written in John's small, neat penmanship.

There was a long "P.S." curling up the side of the paper. She had to turn the sheet in order to read it completely.

"This is just a cover letter (ha! ha!)," it said. "He thought it would be better if I delivered it, in case you were in a bad mood and saw him from your window and tore it up before reading it. So now go ahead and read it and don't pay any attention to what I wrote."

Lori's fingers suddenly felt clammy against the second piece of paper. She let John's letter fall to her lap as she shifted her attention to the second sheet.

"Lori," it said, in the stylized block printing he had perfected that summer at camp. "Am sick too. Aren't colds a drag? Though according to the grapevine, yours is a lot worse than mine. I only missed two days of school, but you've already missed . . . well, you remember how bad I am at math. We have much to discuss, don't you think? Or am I wrong? The logistics of finding and moving bushel baskets of leaves seem overwhelming. We all need your advice. (Don't rip this letter in half! I'm serious!) I will get to you somehow or other."

It was signed in script, the letters large and bold and transforming the brevity of his name into something striking.

At the bottom of the page he had added: "The weather is fine and I wish you were here."

Lori caught herself smiling. There had been one girl at camp that season who kept receiving post-cards everyday from her boyfriend with exactly the same message. The postcards had filled up the wall beside the girl's bunk. She thought they were the most romantic words imaginable. Everyone else thought the guy was totally lacking in imagination. He never varied the message.

Lori reread Ian's note. She didn't know how she was responding to it. Her head seemed too clogged to take in all the shades of meanings in its few lines. She wondered if perhaps she was trying to read too much into it. Perhaps it was just a simple note about the ongoing preparations for the dance.

She folded the two pieces of paper back into the

envelope and placed them on her bedside table. Her eyes went to the hands of the clock. There was more than an hour before her mother would be arriving with a dinner tray.

Her mind was still trying to deal with the underlying theme of Ian's simple note when her mother appeared. Lori didn't even realize until she was halfway through the meal that she was being subjected to another poached egg.

"You have company," Mrs. Kennedy announced. Lori turned with sudden excitement toward her mother. "That is, if you think you're strong enough for company. Do you want to fix your hair or anything? You'll have time while I go downstairs and give the word that you're presentable."

Lori looked across the room at her image in the mirror above her dresser. She didn't look that bad for someone who had been battling both the chills and a fever for the past few days. In fact, the paleness of her face contrasting with her dark hair was rather attractive. If only her nose weren't quite so red!

She was just reaching for her comb when she heard footsteps coming down the hallway. She quickly put the comb back on the bedside table and began adjusting her blanket. When she looked up again, Amanda was standing in the doorway.

"You've got a visitor," the eleven-year-old said.

"I know. Mom already told me."

"Did she tell you who it is?"

"No," Lori said, pushing back a few strands of hair.

"Want to guess?"

"No."

"Colds make you really cranky, don't they?"

Lori adjusted her pillow and ignored her sister.

"I wouldn't get too excited," said Amanda. "And stop fussing with your hair like you thought someone special was coming."

Lori's hand stopped in midair.

"But you don't have to get upset, either," Amanda continued, noticing her sister's reaction. "I mean it's not like it's that stocky little short guy bringing you flowers or something." She paused. "Too bad he didn't show up today. I could have made some extra money bringing you the flowers."

Lori could hear footsteps on the hall carpeting. "Amanda, just get out of here."

"Oh, okay," her sister sighed. "I guess you two have a lot to talk about, and I'd only be in the way. Besides, I don't think I'm much interested in what you might have to say to each other."

"Amanda . . ."

"Gosh, the way you're acting you'd think someone really important was showing up. I mean after all, it's only—"

"It's only me!"

Lori wondered if her face revealed the disappointment she felt inside. Janis was all smiles as she pushed into the room, and Lori was finding it extremely difficult to respond in kind.

"Guess I'll be leaving you guys." Amanda

grinned. "Feel free to talk all that dumb stuff, and don't worry about me standing out in the hallway taking notes."

Janis turned back to Lori, a smile on her face. "Well, anyway, thank goodness your mother finally let me in to see you. Do we have things to talk about!" Janis said, happily settling down on the small chair next to Lori's bed.

Lori felt herself sinking even further back into the pillow. A dull throb was building in both temples, seeking to break through the stuffiness of her congested head. Now she understood why her mother had been turning away friends and denying her the use of the telephone. She wasn't ready for the outside world yet, especially when it arrived in the overwhelming form of Janis Jamison.

"It's going great!" Lori heard Janis say, suddenly realizing that she hadn't been listening to a word coming from the girl's smiling lips. "Everyone's pulling together and adding their own ideas, and best of all—you're not going to believe this!—Mrs. Rinehart really flipped over the basic concept. Who'd have thought she'd go for something like leaves! I mean she's usually so neat and fussy and I thought she might have a fit when I brought up your idea, but she only frowned for about a second and then she started going on and on about the originality of it all, how refreshing it sounded. I felt really sorry for the people working on the interior of the gym. She was really giving them a hard time about the ceiling. I think she seriously wanted them to do something like bring in some real stars for it or at least tear up the roof and let the sky show through. I think that woman is starting to change right before our eyes. She sounds as if she's going to be open to really wild ideas from now on. John thinks we might be able to get away with real snowbanks and icicles for the winter dance. Of course, he's crazy, but who knows . . ."

The throb in Lori's forehead was growing in intensity. Janis continued to talk about the decorations for the dance. Lori wondered if she should tell her friend that it was all falling on deaf, clogged ears. She even doubted if she could keep her eyes open much longer. Janis' voice was acting as a sedative on her already fogged mind.

"And it's Ian who's really added all the great touches."

Lori felt something run through her body at the mention of his name. She was amazed that it only took those two syllables to revive her.

"He wants to build a real stone wall along the hall leading to the door. He says it should add to the effect of the entrance to the gym itself. Something about the gateway to a magic kingdom. He's charmed Mrs. Rinehart into that idea too, which is incredible considering how much that woman used to believe in paint and paper. Inside the gym she's even letting them use actual haystacks! John wants to bring up the possibility of having some real horses. I don't think she's going to buy that idea, but who knows . . .? Anyway, you don't have to worry about the committee. Ian and I have things under control and waiting for you to get back. Everything's running smoothly."

Janis had been standing next to the bed while she

talked, but now she lowered herself onto the edge of the mattress and her smile disappeared. "But then there's the important stuff," she said, running her hand along the blanket. "We really need you back in action, Lori. We really do. Everything seems to have come to a complete standstill without your advice. It's like we're all waiting for you to start things happening again."

The throb, which had vanished from Lori's forehead for a few seconds, came back with renewed strength. She glanced at the glass of water next to her bed and reached for it. The liquid tasted warm and stale, but she drank it all, glad to concentrate on its progress down her throat.

There was no way that she could completely block out the words coming from Janis, who proceeded to give detailed accounts of the accumulation of problems that Lori was expected to deal with once she returned to school. Janis hinted that it would be helpful if Lori could pass along some of her expertise even from her sickbed. "We really need you," Janis kept saying. "None of us knows what to do."

Lori answered finally with a heavy, throat-clogging sigh.

"What's the matter?" Janis asked.

"I still feel awful," Lori said, sniffing to add emphasis to her words. "This cold has really drained me of energy."

"Oh." Janis sounded disappointed.

"I'm glad things are going so well with the committee," Lori said, adding a convincing cough for good measure.

"The committee's going great," Janis conceded. "It's just everything else that's . . . well, I already explained how things stand in that department."

"When are we going to get the stones and the leaves?" Lori asked, reaching for her glass once again and lifting it to her lips despite the fact that she had already drained it completely earlier.

"Ian and John have already taken care of the stones. As for the leaves, we'll see to them the day before we start the decorating," Janis said. "You'll be back by then, won't you?"

"I hope so." Lori choked out another cough and then brought her hand up to her hair. "It's up to my mother I guess," she said, tucking some unwashed strands behind her ear. "I was pretty sick for awhile and she wants me to be careful."

Janis stood up. "Maybe I should be going," she said. "I don't want to tire you out so that you have a relapse or anything."

"I'm sorry," Lori said.

"Sorry?"

"About getting sick and not being able to deal with . . . well, you know."

Janis smiled. "Oh, don't worry," she said. "You'll get your strength back and then you'll come to our rescue again. We can all hold on a little bit longer, though I sometimes wonder if John and I will ever get things exactly right. I mean, it's not that we're not friendly or anything like that, it's just that the relationship lacks . . . I don't know . . . fireworks or something. It's just sort of . . . sort of unexciting. It's definitely not like you and Ian! You two really know how to set the sparks flying. I'd give anything to have that kind of . . . well, anyway, we all do need your help, so try and get better as quickly as possible so that . . . well, I guess I'll just tell the other girls that you're still sick and that they'll just have to wait."

"Maybe they should try to figure things out for themselves and—"

"No, we need you."

"But I'm not as great an expert as—"

"Oh, stop being so modest. You're just saying that because you have a cold and aren't feeling well. Once you're well, you'll realize how brilliant you are on these matters."

"But—"

"But nothing, Lori. Now calm down and get some rest and we'll all see you in a few days. We'll turn that leaf-hunting expedition into something special. Now just get your rest and maybe your mother will let me visit again another time."

Janis began moving towards the door. "Oh," she said, coming to an abrupt halt and reaching into her blouse pocket. "I almost forgot to give you this." She withdrew a folded piece of paper and tossed it to Lori. "Some messenger service I am!" she added. She waved good-by to Lori and left the room.

Lori looked down at the note in her lap. Her fingers reached for the paper slowly, as if deliberately wanting to draw out the excitement she was feeling.

"Dear Lori," she read after unfolding the sheet of paper. "Will be in touch. Get better. Ian."

Lori's hand crumpled up the note. That was all?

It was for those few lines that she had gotten so excited? She tossed the paper at the basket next to her desk. It missed and she struggled out of bed and picked it up angrily; then she smoothed it out on the desktop, turning it over several times to make sure she hadn't missed anything. All she found was the same message and lots of white space.

Lori had a hard time falling asleep that night. Every time she thought she was just about to nod off, the window would rattle and wake her once again.

She finally decided to switch on the light and read for awhile. Instead of producing drowsiness, however, the book woke her up even more. She was surprised when she glanced at the clock and discovered how late it was. She shut the book and put it back on the bedside table, wondering if perhaps her head wasn't beginning to feel a little better. She sensed that she was truly on the road to complete recovery, and yet that possibility didn't really delight her as much as it should have. Her mother would make her return to school, and then everything would just start all over again, and . . .

The window rattled again and this time she got out of bed and slammed it shut. If she was getting better, then it wouldn't hurt for one night to do without Mother's dose of clean, fresh air. Sleep was more important, and that rattling window was—

A shadowy movement caught her eye as she looked down into the yard. The street lights didn't reach that side of the house and it was extremely dark, but she was sure she saw something moving.

It was difficult to see clearly because the window reflected the room itself, lit up as it was by the lamp beside her bed. She went back to the table, turned off the lamp, and returned to the window. Yes, there was definitely something moving down there, something moving back and forth with deliberation. But the shadows were too thick and bushes obscured part of her field of vision, so she couldn't make out anything clearly. She raised the window an inch or so and listened. The sound of rustling leaves came from below.

The neighbor's dog, she thought. Her mother had suspected the dog of making nocturnal visits before in search of treasures he had probably been burying for years on their property. There was one spot near the chimney that was particularly subject to freshly dug holes, and Mrs. Kennedy had been trying to think of diplomatic ways to approach their rather standoffish neighbor about the matter. To-night, the noise coming from below sounded as if the dog was on its most elaborate treasure hunt ever.

Lori closed the window again and crawled back into bed. She shut her eyes and still didn't feel tired. Not that it mattered. Her mother was not going to let her return to school tomorrow, and she could sleep all morning.

Her ears picked up the rustling from the lawn once again. That dog seemed to be having a great time.

She was still awake when the sounds from below ceased. The wind that had been rattling the window also died away, and Lori had nothing to listen to but the silence of the night.

"Hey, lazybones, it's a beautiful morning and the temperature's threatening to break all records for this time of the year." Lori sat up and looked at her mother. "You look better, too. Why don't you come downstairs and have breakfast in the kitchen? There are still some waffles left if you're in the mood for something hearty."

Lori suddenly felt extremely hungry, hungrier than she had been for days. Her head seemed remarkably free of congestion, and the idea of breakfast had enormous appeal for her.

"Why don't you get dressed quickly and I'll warm up the waffle iron. Do you want one or two?" Mrs. Kennedy smiled as Lori held up three fingers. "We'll see how you handle two," she said with a laugh. "And while you're getting dressed, take a look out the window and see what's happened to the lawn."

Lori pushed back the bedcovers and started getting up. "I thought that dog was having a fieldday last night," she said, moving toward her dresser.

"Dog?"

"From next door. I could hear him digging about. I guess it's time you had a talk with Mrs. Thomas, or we may not have any lawn left."

Mrs. Kennedy laughed. "I don't think Mrs.

Thomas is the one to talk to about what happened to our lawn last night. Just go and take a look for yourself while I'm seeing to your waffles."

Lori picked out some clothes from the dresser drawer and placed them on her bed. After breakfast, she was going to take a long shower and wash her hair and then maybe sit outside and read and . . .

She drifted to the window and looked out. The midmorning sun shone brightly into her eyes and she had to squint to see below.

She didn't take it in at first, but then suddenly the scene came into focus.

A large cardboard sign was dangling from the branch below her head. The letters were somewhat blurred because the sign was swaying in the light breeze, but she could still make out the words displayed in a familiar block print:

JUST CAN'T LEAF YOU ALONE!

Are you sure you're up to this?" Janis asked, pulling one of the bushel baskets from the back of the station wagon. "I mean, it's only your first day back at school and I don't want you to have a relapse from overexerting yourself."

"I'm fine, Janis," Lori said. "I could have come back yesterday if my mother hadn't made me get checked out by the doctor. He said I'm in perfect shape."

Janis didn't seem convinced. "What's-his-name came back too quickly and he's out again," she said. "But I guess you noticed that."

Yes, Lori was fully aware of the fact that Ian hadn't been in school that day. She had searched for his blond head in the halls from early morning on, only to be told at lunch by a girl at her table that he had been missing from classes ever since the day after he had left the message on Lori's lawn.

"Well, if you start getting tired," Janis said, pulling the last basket from the car, "just go and sit down to rest and we'll all understand."

"I'm fine, Janis!" Lori insisted again. "And this has to be done today, so that we can start work tomorrow inside."

Janis slammed the trunk door shut. "Where's my mother gotten to?" she asked.

A nearby girl pointed further into the park where they could make out Mrs. Jamison's ample form heading toward the pavilion near the lake.

"Okay," Janis said. "Let's divide up into pairs and get this drudgery over with. And remember, we want *colorful* leaves, so don't settle for too many dreary brown ones. That gym hallway is gloomy enough without adding to its ugliness. You come with me, Lori. We have to talk."

Everyone grabbed several baskets and began moving off into the wooded section of the park. Lori followed Janis. It felt good to be out in the crisp fall air, and she didn't even mind the fact that Janis obviously wanted to discuss personal matters.

"Well," Janis said, reaching an embankment of yellow leaves and tossing her basket to the ground. "I finally got John to come out and ask me to the dance and you know what he said? He said that he had just assumed that we were going together. Assumed! Do you believe that! What is wrong with that boy?"

Lori felt a sinking sensation in her chest. Through all the turmoil of the last few weeks, she herself had been making the same assumption, but the reality of the situation was that Ian had never even brought up the matter. Had *he* been assuming the same thing, or was there the possibility that she was actually lacking a date for the dance?

She felt her lips twisting into an awkward smile as Janis went on and on about John's lack of finesse. Janis didn't really seem to want her to say anything yet. She just wanted to spill over about everything that had or hadn't happened since Lori had become ill, and Lori found herself listening with only half an ear. She almost felt like telling Janis to stop chattering, that she had her own problems. After all, Janis *had* a date for the dance.

"So I told him he'd better not be so sure of himself in the future," Janis said, leaning over and stuffing some of the leaves into one of the baskets. "And then you know what happened? He said that if he couldn't assume things about me, then maybe I shouldn't assume things about him, and that there were lots of girls who liked . . ."

Lori wasn't listening at all now. She scooped up leaves quickly, tamped them down into her bushel basket until it was full, and then reached for another one. The thought came to her that if Ian was still sick by the next Saturday, she was definitely dateless. She would have to go home after last-minute decorating to spend the night in her own room, while everyone else enjoyed the fruits of her labor. What an irony that would be! Advice Goddess of Lincoln High all by her lonesome, while the rest of the world partied!

"So what do you think? Did I do the right thing?" Janis asked.

Lori looked up with a start. She didn't know what the question was referring to. She gave Janis what she thought was an encouraging smile.

"You really think that was the right thing to say? He's been awfully cool to me since then and he made up some flimsy excuse about why he couldn't help us out today," Janis babbled as she pushed a final handful of leaves into her basket. "Well, I guess if you think it will work in the long run." She smiled weakly. "I don't know about John, though."

"You don't know about *John?*" a girl said from behind Lori. "What about me and Michael? Now that's something that really needs working on."

Before Lori could respond, the girl went into a long, involved explanation of her relationship with the boy. None of it sounded familiar to Lori, and yet from the way that the girl spoke, it was obvious that at one time she, Lori, had passed on some advice to her. The girl's face was only vaguely familiar, and Lori searched her mind in vain for a name to attach to the long-haired blonde before her. An odd sensation began to grow within her. How could she have presumed to hand out advice to a complete stranger?

"But was that a good move?" the blonde asked. "It seemed to be, at the time, but now I'm not so sure. Have you ever gone through anything like that?"

Lori realized that she hadn't been listening closely to the girl. "Well, what exactly happened?"

she said, hoping an explanation would be forth-coming.

"Just as I told you," the girl said sadly. "He didn't even bother to take it back and exchange it and . . . well, you can see how the situation stands now. It's all pretty weird."

Lori didn't have the faintest idea what the girl was talking about. "Don't worry," she said. "Things will become less weird."

"They will?" the girl said. "But don't I have to do something to make that come about?"

"Just play it by ear," said Lori.

"By ear? You mean wait until he says something first and then if it's nasty, say something nasty back to him? Is that what you mean?"

"No, not exactly," Lori replied. "You don't have to be nasty. In fact, why don't you be nice in-stead?"

"Nice?"

"Sure," Lori said, all the while wondering why she was bothering to offer advice so blindly. "Nice-ness never hurts."

"Do you think that's what I should try too?" Janis asked.

"Each person and each relationship is different," Lori said, sounding extremely pompous to herself. She felt as though she were standing outside her own body and listening to a girl she didn't under-stand at all.

Another girl had stopped gathering leaves and joined them. Lori sensed that the newcomer was about to inject yet another set of romantic prob-lems into the conversation.

"I'm still not sure what you think I should do," the blonde said.

Lori looked at her watch quickly. "Don't you think we should concentrate on getting the baskets full before it gets late?" she said, leaning down and digging her hand into a pile of fallen leaves. "There'll be lots more time to talk about other things later on."

"But the dance is only a few days away," the newcomer said. "We need your help now so that—" She broke off in midsentence as her eyes caught sight of someone over Lori's shoulder. "I thought he was sick," she said to no one in particular.

"If that's what sick looks like, then I wish Michael would catch cold immediately," sighed the blonde.

"Come on girls," Janis said, giving Lori a conspiratorial wink. "I think a certain person might like to be left alone with a certain other person."

Lori swung her head around in the direction they were all staring. She felt herself blushing. Ian was only about twenty feet away, his long legs carrying him slowly up toward them through the trees.

The other girls disappeared up the embankment, leaving Lori standing alone with the baskets. She tried to will the blush out of her cheeks, but she felt her face growing even warmer as he came to a halt in front of her.

"Ssh!" he said, raising a finger to his lips. "Don't tell anyone I'm here. Technically speaking, I'm home in bed suffering from the renewed vengeance of an ungrateful cold." He coughed. "You're looking good," he said. "I take it you're fully recovered."

Lori nodded. "But you're not," she said with concern. "Why in the world have you come out here today?"

Ian shrugged. "I was getting cabin fever and decided I needed some fresh air. And besides, my parents won't be back home 'til late, and what they don't know can't hurt them."

"But it can hurt their son, being out here when he should be resting at home in bed."

"Oh, don't worry about me," he laughed hoarsely. "Seeing you is better medicine than bed rest anyway."

"You're not dressed very warmly," she observed.

"It's a lot warmer than it looks," he said, fingering his wool sweater. "Especially in the sun."

"There's no sun here," she said.

"Then maybe I'd better get to work and make sure I keep warm that way." He bent down and began picking up handfuls of leaves and depositing them in one of the nearby baskets. "Are we getting only yellow today?" he said, holding up a single leaf.

"There are lots of orange ones down that way," she replied, leaning over next to him and beginning to fill an empty container. "Don't worry—our collection will be the brightest of them all."

"But no red ones." He filled his bushel basket to the top and then stood up. "So," he said, "are you getting excited about the big dance?"

"Are you?"

"I'm not sure yet. It could be fun, I guess, if you go with the right person. My friend's been wondering if the right person would want to go with him."

Lori didn't look up. She continued gathering leaves in her hands and tossing them into the basket. The woods seemed very silent except for the sound of her movements as she dug into the piles of leaves over the mossy soil.

"He's not even sure how to ask her," Ian said, bringing his hand up to his mouth to stifle a cough. "She'd probably just laugh."

"He'll never know until he tries," Lori said softly.

"What was that?" he asked.

"He'll never know until he tries," she repeated loudly enough to surprise herself.

"Oh," he said. "No, I guess he won't until he does. It's just that he's so afraid of being shot down." Ian tried to laugh, but his throat would only allow another cough to burst forth. "But you think he should risk it, huh?"

"He'd better not wait too long," Lori said, a trace of irritation in her voice. "The dance is only a few days away and she might not appreciate being asked on such short notice. She's got her pride, you know. Besides, she might already have agreed to go with someone else."

"You think she already has a date?"

"Could be," Lori said. "If she's as sophisticated as you say she is, then I'm sure she has her pick of dates."

Why in the world was she talking like that when it only worked to her disadvantage? She wished he would come right out and ask her and stop playing games.

"Well, if she's already got a date, then maybe he won't even bother to ask," Ian said, his foot tapping against the wood of one of the baskets.

"He'll never know then, will he?" Lori said with a trace of anger.

"You're big on advice today, aren't you? Is that some of the expertise they're all so eager to get hold of around here?" Ian kicked at the basket at his feet. He misjudged the force of his movement, and the container toppled over, spilling its leaves as it started to roll down the embankment. He stood in silence, watching its descent until it came to a rest next to the trunk of a tree.

"Well," he said, "no use crying over spilled . . . leaves."

"No," she concurred, picking up her own basket and starting back to the car. If he couldn't even get out a simple invitation, she was darned if she would beg for it.

10

No! No! That's all wrong!" Mrs. Rinehart called up to some of the boys on the scaffolding. "You can't even see the stars from below if they're hanging that way. Do them all over again and try to remember that they are meant to be for the benefit of the dancers, not for free-floating astronauts."

Janis pulled Lori back to the gym wall and let out a groan. "She's in a terrible mood, isn't she?"

"She's right though. The stars have to be hung a certain way."

"Do you think she'll want us hung a certain way when she discovers the fiasco waiting for her in the hall?" Janis asked grimly.

"It's not that bad."

"You're right," Janis said. "It's not that bad. It's just not anything at all. It's just . . . a mess of leaves."

"We'll get it right. We just need to distance ourselves from it for awhile by taking a break."

"Oh, no!" Janis whispered. "She just spotted us. She's going to think we came in here to tell her that we're finished, and after she sees the hall, we sure are going to be finished. They won't let us near the art department ever again."

"Calm down, Janis. She's still dealing with all the problems in the gym. By the time she's ready to inspect the entrance, we'll have . . . Oh, no! You're right! She's heading our way!"

"It needs work, girls," Mrs. Rinehart said. "Where's the rest of your committee, anyway? Are they all tired from leaf-picking?"

"I gave them a break," Lori said. "They'll all be back in a half hour and then we'll—"

"And then you'll put into action the plan that was presented to me originally? Or have you discarded that completely?"

"Well, no," Janis said. "It's just that—"

"I'll come back later to see that marvelous lighting effect you promised," Mrs. Rinehart said. "In the meanwhile, you'd better settle down to work. I don't see much going on here."

Janis raised her eyes as Mrs. Rinehart vanished into the gym. "What are we going to do?" she sighed. "What's-his-name had worked out all of the lighting and now . . . well, how were we to know that he was going to get sick again."

"We'll just have to do it ourselves."

"How, Lori? I'm not even sure exactly what he was talking about. It just sounded good and Mrs.

Rinehart kept looking happy and . . . oh, what have we gotten ourselves into?"

"Nothing that we can't deal with."

"Maybe we should give him a call on the phone and—"

"Janis, we'll deal with it."

The next time Mrs. Rinehart poked her head out the door, there was a series of lamps hanging against the wall. She held up her arm to ward off the overpowering brightness of the lighting.

"Is this what we had in mind?" she asked.

"Oh, no, Mrs. Rinehart," Janis assured her. "We're still working on perfecting it. This is just sort of a rough sketch."

"A rough sketch," Mrs. Rinehart repeated, dazed. She peered down the length of the hallway. "Where's that tall, blond boy gotten to?" she asked.

"He's out ill," Janis said.

"Aren't most of these ideas his?"

"Not all of them. In fact most of them are hers." Janis pointed to Lori with pride. "She came up with the original plan for using the leaves and everything, but then she got sick and Ian and I sort of had to take over for awhile."

"You certainly aren't a very healthy crew, are you?" Mrs. Rinehart said. She looked down the hallway again. "Where's that short boy with the dark hair? The one who claimed he was a born electrician."

"He can't get here 'til tonight," Janis explained. "He had a very important appointment."

"An appointment?"

"He's being fitted for his tuxedo."

"Tuxedo? I had no idea this dance was going to be so formal."

"Well, he thought it would be fun to wear one," Janis said.

Mrs. Rinehart stared down at the bushel baskets of leaves lining the hallway and raised an eyebrow. Several of the students started to laugh.

"I think it's a very original idea," Janis said defensively. "I had no trouble at all talking him into it."

"All right, settle down and get back to work," said Mrs. Rinehart. "Why shouldn't he wear a tuxedo if he wants to? I think it's encouraging that at least one of you youngsters knows there is more to life than jeans."

Lori drew closer to Janis' side. "You really talked John into wearing a tuxedo?"

"Well, that's what you told me to do!" Janis snapped back.

"I did?"

"Of course you did. Stop acting so dumb and let's see if we can figure out how to get those lights glowing mysteriously under the leaves without burning the whole school to the ground."

"How come we haven't seen Mrs. Rinehart in a while?" Janis asked one of the committee members.

"Didn't you hear? She decided to go out for dinner instead of raiding the machines in the cafeteria like the rest of us. I think she needed to get away for awhile. The stars still aren't hanging right."

Lori bit into her apple and surveyed the hallway. The lamps weren't hanging right either, and one of them was already broken. Nothing was turning out the way she had expected it to. Half the leaves were being crumpled into fine bits and the place looked as though a storm had just passed through.

Laura Cooper came out of the gym and peered down the row of unhappy faces against the far wall. Her eyes focused as they found Lori. "Boy, do I need to see you," she said, coming forward. "He won't listen to a word I'm saying. He's got this idea that I've been flirting all afternoon with Kenny Mailer and nothing will get it out of his head. What should I do, Lori? If he keeps acting like this, the dance is going to be awful for me."

Lori had an uncontrollable urge to yawn in Laura's face. She was tired and discouraged and she really didn't want to deal with anyone else's problems at the moment. "What do you think you should do?"

"What do *I* think I should do? I want to know what *you* think. You must have been through something like this before. I need your help."

"Tell him that you have the right to flirt with anyone you want," Lori said.

"But I wasn't flirting!"

"Well, tell him that then."

"You haven't been listening," Laura said with a discouraged look. "I already told him that."

"Well then, tell him he's a jerk," Lori said with a sigh.

Laura Cooper pulled back slightly. "I can't tell him that. I love the guy." She frowned slightly and then a growing brightness appeared in her eyes. "Do you think maybe I could get away with it?"

"You'll never know 'til you try it," Lori said blithely.

"I don't know—it's the sort of thing that might backfire on me." She drew in a breath of air. "But then again, your advice hasn't failed me in the past. I never would have gotten together with him in the first place if it hadn't been for you. Thanks, Lori. I'm going to try it."

Janis was still open-mouthed after Laura had left. "Did I hear that whole conversation right?" she asked. "You told her to tell him that he was a jerk?"

Lori nodded as she looked around for some place to toss the half-eaten apple.

"You know, Lori, sometimes lately I think your advice is a little . . . well, maybe it's a little too frank for Lincoln High."

"Do you think enough light would show through the openings in the baskets if we put the lamps under them and scattered the leaves on top?" Lori asked, ignoring her friend's comment.

Janis thought the matter over for a few seconds. "You know what I really think," she said. "I think that if one of us doesn't make a phone call soon, we're going to be in big trouble."

"Stop worrying. We don't need Ian Winslow's help to work out our problems."

Janis stared directly into Lori's face. "That's another thing I've been meaning to talk to you about. Ever since my party, you two have been acting really strange with each other. I'm beginning to wonder—are you two really not getting along?"

"How about if we try one of the lamps under a basket just to see how it works out," Lori said with sudden enthusiasm. "Come on, people. We can whip this place into shape if we give it a final effort!"

"So you think I should pretend I like his brother and that way he'll get jealous and finally ask me?" The girl sounded a little dubious about Lori's suggestion.

"Yes, that's just the thing to do," Lori said, as she tried to keep a pile of leaves from falling away from the wall.

"Are you sure?"

"Have I failed anyone yet?"

"Well, no, but his brother is only thirteen years old. Won't it seem a little funny if—"

"Just trust me."

"Okay, if you say so."

"Now would you please go and get me one of those spray bottles. Maybe if I mist things with some water . . ."

"Well, where have you been?" Janis said crossly.

"You know where I've been." There was a look of confusion on John's face. It wasn't the greeting he had expected. "Wait 'til you see it," he said, managing a smile. "It's going to look really nifty."

"Nifty? Where do you get those words anyway?"

Janis shoved a basket of leaves into John's hands. "We all know it's going to look ridiculous."

"Ridiculous!"

"It was a dumb idea to begin with."

"It was *your* idea to begin with," John said angrily. "And who says it's going to look ridiculous."

"Everyone's going to be laughing at us."

"Says who?"

"They've already been laughing."

"Who's been laughing? What are you talking about?"

"You shouldn't have let her talk you into it."

"Her?"

"Lori. It was her idea in the first place."

"It was?"

"Well, I sort of thought it up, but she's the one who gave me the go ahead. And now we're going to be the laughingstock of Lincoln High, and it's all her fault. And yours, too."

"What!"

"And just look at this place! Why did I ever think it would be fun to be on the decorating committee this year! This is an utter disaster!"

"Tell your mother that if you can't go, you're quitting high school and running away to New York."

"I'd never do anything that drastic."

"Take my word for it. It's a surefire solution to all your problems. Your mother will be greeting him with open arms in no time at all."

"My mother hates him. She says if I see him again—"

"Listen, I've told you what you should do. Now could you please just move a little to the right. That's it. Now try to hold that leaf in place 'til the glue dries."

"Let me just go outside and come in again," Lori said. "Maybe if I see it from the point of view of someone arriving for the dance, I'll be able to figure out what details aren't working."

"None of them are working," Janis said under her breath.

"Everybody just keep arranging those big yellow leaves," Lori shouted as she made her way to the door. "And please try not to break any more of the lamps. Tread carefully, people."

The cold evening air did little to clear her head. In a few moments she was shivering, but she remained on the gym steps anyway, dreading the return to the leaf-strewn corridor she had been trapped in for hours. She leaned against one of the pillars next to the door and closed her eyes and tried to blot out everything.

"You trying to have a relapse too?"

She turned with a start to find Ian standing close behind her.

They didn't say anything for a few moments. She was too busy trying to sort out all the mixed feelings rising inside her.

"I thought you were—"

"I was. I mean, I still am, a little bit."

"Then why are you here?" she asked, drawing her arms together as her shivering increased.

"I thought you might . . . you might need me. I was lying there in bed and it suddenly struck me that I might not ever have really explained to you how the lamps were to be set up, and I thought of giving you a call, and then I decided, what the heck, it won't kill me to drop by for awhile and see if you needed a helping hand."

"We do need you," Lori said simply.

He looked relieved. "Then I guess it was a good idea to come."

Lori smiled at him. "Are you sure you really want to go inside? It's been a total disaster so far," she admitted.

"It can't be that bad."

"It is. I'm a complete failure at decorating gym hallways."

Ian laughed.

"Remember how good I was at decorating the pavilion at Camp Maplewood? Well, I guess I've lost that talent completely since then."

"Stop being so hard on yourself."

"Just promise you won't laugh too hard when you go through that door."

"Oh, hush. Come on, let's get in there and do what needs doing, instead of freezing out here on these dumb steps." His hand reached for the door and he began pulling it open. "After you, Ms. Kennedy," he said.

"Maybe I'll just go home and let you take over."

"Lori, would you just hush up and get in there?

We've got work to do and I don't think I can do much on my own."

"You mean you need me?" she said.

"Right." He smiled. "I need my old camp buddy."

She looked up at him and tried to find the boy she had known those many summers ago. There seemed fewer traces of that boy tonight, and yet she was afraid to start searching the thin planes of his face for the signs of maturity she so longed to find. At the moment, she had more pressing problems—such as what to do about decorating the gym.

11

Now this is more like it!" Mrs. Rinehart was actually smiling as she moved down the hallway and turned to inspect the effect of the changes from a distance. "In fact, this is how I had it explained to me." She glanced at Ian. "I didn't think we were going to see you around here tonight, young man."

"We just lucked out, Mrs. Rinehart," Janis said.

Some of the other students nodded in agreement.

"The lighting is spectacular," the teacher continued. "Spectacular."

"We have John to thank for that," Ian said.

"I couldn't have done it if you hadn't showed me where to—"

"Stop being so modest. He's a real expert with wiring."

"Well, it's just marvelous," Mrs. Rinehart enthused. "And the way the leaves reach up around the doorway—are they going to stay that way until tomorrow night?"

"Sure," Ian said. "Lori figured out a way to glue them to some wire mesh. Those side piles are actually hollow inside, but who's going to know the difference?"

"Well, it's all lovely. I knew things would come together once you gave it that extra effort."

Lori herself was amazed at how things had fallen into place. It only took Ian's presence to get the ball rolling. He made a few suggestions and suddenly everyone seemed to be coming up with workable ideas. It was almost as if they had all come awake upon his arrival.

"I guess I can go home tonight and not worry anymore about this part of the gym," said Mrs. Rinehart, casting an unhappy eye toward the door leading to the interior.

"Yes," Janis said. "We can all rest easy tonight. I mean, once you reach perfection, what else is there to do but rest easy?"

"It's not perfect yet," said Ian.

"It's not? It looks perfect to me."

"No, there's something missing."

"What do you mean?"

Ian's eyes traveled along the hallway. "I'm not sure," he said. "But it lacks something."

Mrs. Rinehart actually laughed. "Well, I'm sure that by tomorrow night you'll have figured out just what that something is." She looked at her wristwatch. "I think all of us could use a good night's sleep. There's always tomorrow afternoon for finishing touches. I'm going in there to tell the rest of the students that it's time to call it quits. See you all tomorrow."

"I think we really impressed her," Janis said as she reached for her jacket. "And I know I'm impressed by what we've accomplished. Ian's brilliant. That's all there is to it."

"Yeah, Ian's really talented," said John. "Super-talented."

"Would you guys stop it? I'm no more talented than the rest of you."

"Stop kidding yourself," Janis laughed.

"Yes, stop kidding yourself," Lori said. "From now on you shouldn't be hiding your talents—"

"—under a bushel basket!" everyone shouted, laughing.

Ian held up his hands as if warding off their compliments. "Quick, Lori, let's get out of here before I start to believe what they're saying. There's nothing worse than an artist with a swelled head." His hands dropped. "I mean, there's nothing worse than a . . . a guy with a swelled head," he added awkwardly.

"No," said Lori. "You got it right the first time."

She was surprised that he didn't bristle at her words. Instead he gave her his shy smile. "Well, maybe," he said finally. "At least we'll see."

Everyone began moving out onto the gym steps. The chilly autumn night came as a shock to many of them after they'd spent so many hours in the overheated hallway. Yet no one seemed to want to disperse quickly. They were all still enjoying the afterglow of having worked together well, and they didn't want to break the mood.

The door was suddenly pulled open roughly, and a boy pushed his way through the crowd, followed moments later by an unhappy-looking girl.

"But what about my ride?" she called out after him.

"Go find someone else with a car!" he yelled back. "Go find a *real* jerk!"

The girl was on the point of tears. She turned back to the door and spotted Lori. "A lot of help you've been," she said angrily. "He's never going to talk to me again as long as I live!"

She reached for the door handle, only to be pushed aside by another couple exiting the building.

"So you like my brother! So go to the dance with him! See if I care!"

"Be serious. He's just a kid."

"He's big for his age. You'd only have to stoop a little to put your head on his shoulder during the slow numbers. Go ahead and give him a call right now. Tell him I told you it was okay, that you're certainly not my girl any longer."

"I'm not?"

"Not by a long shot."

The girl came to a halt while the boy kept walking. She turned forlornly to the steps as he disappeared into the darkness. "Great!" she said loudly to no one in particular. "Just what I need! A date with a thirteen-year-old!" Her eyes focused in on Lori. "Thanks for the advice," she said sarcastically. "The results have been more than I ever would have expected. You really have a knack with these things, don't you?"

Lori tried to avoid the embarrassed looks of everyone on the steps. She had been feeling so happy, and now it was all being destroyed by . . .

The door swung open again, and Lori cringed as she recognized the girl coming out onto the steps. The girl cast a sad look at her and said nothing. Everyone else had fallen silent, obviously expecting another outburst.

"You want to get out of here?" Ian asked. He brought his arm up protectively to her shoulder. "Come on, I'll walk you home."

"Home?" the sad-eyed girl said. She looked around mournfully at the students on the gym steps. "I suppose all of you will be going home soon, won't you?" She paused and gulped loudly. "Home," she repeated. "A place I guess I'll never see again." Her eyes locked with Lori's. "You think you could lend me some money?" she said. "I didn't exactly come prepared with enough cash to get to New York tonight. And I'll need some loose change for the taxi that I'll have to hire to pick up my bags from . . . well, at least they're already packed and waiting for me, according to my mother. Or so she told me a few minutes ago over the phone when I put your surefire advice into action. I must say this—it certainly got results. I'll be thinking of you when I'm starving to death in some cold-water tenement that I'll be forced to call . . . home."

Someone let out a titter at the girl's last sentence, but no one else picked up the laughter. A feeling of tension was spreading through the group, and Lori knew that they were waiting for her to say something.

But before she could open her mouth, the door opened again and a whole stream of students began moving out onto the steps. Several of the girls in the group glared at Lori, and then a few of them began talking at once. The next thing Lori knew, the entire group of students erupted into a chorus of complaints.

The afternoon and evening had obviously been a disaster for boy-girl relationships at Lincoln High, and Lori's glib advice was being blamed for it all. It got to the point where she couldn't listen anymore. She was too busy trying to control the tears building up in her eyes. All the friendships she had started to form were disintegrating before her on those steps. Even Janis voiced her disappointment at the latest turn of events in her love life.

And then suddenly Lori realized that no one was talking. Everyone was looking at her for some kind of response. There was expectation in their faces, almost as if they were hoping she would say something to set everything right once again.

She heard herself clear her throat. She didn't have the faintest idea of how to answer them. Her mouth opened and she was amazed that words started coming out.

"I'm sorry," she said. "Sorry that things aren't working out for most of you. I guess I'm not the right person to be giving advice." She paused and looked at the faces turned to her. "I'm nowhere near as wise as you think I am. My reputation started by accident, and for a while the things I told you were just common sense. Then, when things started going so well, I suppose I started thinking I really did have a talent for guiding other people's lives. That's when I started moving beyond common sense and . . . well, you see what happened."

The faces staring up at her looked as though they still expected more. She cleared her throat again, and now she knew exactly what she wanted to say.

"I just wish that all of you would learn to listen to your own selves a little more. Most of your problems can be solved if you just face them honestly, instead of trying to tackle them with complicated solutions someone else comes up with. Use your own common sense."

She could tell that her words were being greeted with disappointment, that no one really wanted to hear what she was trying to say. It saddened her that now that she was giving the only advice she truly believed in, they seemed to be deaf to it.

"Maybe by tomorrow everything will get straightened out," Lori said.

"Maybe by tomorrow I'll be going to the dance with a thirteen-year-old," a disgruntled female voice said.

"That's better than not even having a jerk to escort you."

"And it's a lot better than being in New York getting ready to starve to death."

"Or arriving at the gym with someone dressed up like a penguin," Janis mumbled.

"Haven't any of you been listening to her?" Ian interrupted. "She's finally starting to make sense, and yet all of you still sound as if you're waiting for her to recapture her phony powers and start handing out magical solutions."

"But she was so good at it at the beginning," Janis sighed.

"It was all common sense," Lori said.

"It didn't seem that common."

"It's inside all of you, if you'd only try to search for it," said Ian, a hoarseness returning to his voice.

"But it's so much easier to have someone else tell you what to do."

"And look at the mess it's made of all your lives," Ian countered.

The people on the steps still didn't seem very happy with what they were hearing, but they were becoming resigned to the fact that no further advice would be offered that night. Individuals began moving slowly away toward the sidewalk.

"So," Ian said, "I guess that's that."

"Do you think I have any friends left around here?"

"You've got me," said John. "You never gave me any bad advice at all. And I still like the idea of the tuxedo."

"You do?" Janis said. "You know that was really my idea. Ridiculous, I know, but at the time I thought it had possibilities."

"It still does," insisted John.

"Well, I must admit I do like a guy in a tuxedo, but if everyone's going to laugh . . ."

"No one will laugh. You two won't laugh, will you?"

Ian coughed. "I think a tux at a barn dance is really sharp," he said. "They won't be able to take their eyes off of you."

"That's what I'm afraid of," said Janis.

"Maybe I like being noticed."

"You do?"

"There's nothing wrong in standing out in a crowd. In fact, it might be nifty."

"There he goes again with that word! Come on, John. Walk me home and we'll decide how we're going to get away with this." Her eyes went to Lori. "And don't worry. You're still my friend. I always suspected you weren't as brilliant as you seemed. It's kind of a relief in a way. It puts us on a more equal footing."

Lori and Ian stood on the deserted steps and watched their friends cut across the school lawn to the next street. Ian's arm was still around her shoulder and she was grateful for the warmth of his nearness.

"Let's get you home," he said, breaking out into a cough once again. "You've had a rough night of it."

"Nothing I won't survive," said Lori, trying to laugh. "You sound in worse shape than I am."

"I guess I haven't shaken it completely," Ian said.

"I think you probably need more rest. You shouldn't have rushed out to come to our rescue."

"I shouldn't have?"

"Your mother's going to be upset."

"What about you? Are you upset?"

"About tonight? No, I'm starting to calm down. I'll be okay. I feel relieved, actually."

"Yeah, so do I."

She looked at him curiously.

"You know how I felt about all those people running after you for advice and the position you were put in," he explained.

"You mean the position I put myself in."

"Well, there might be some truth in that," he admitted. "But we all put ourselves in false positions from time to time."

"Even you?" she laughed.

"You know, I really enjoyed working on that committee. Even though I was feeling lousy."

"That was obvious," said Lori. "It was exciting to watch. I felt as if I was back at camp and you were dragging me down to the lake to sketch the sunrise."

"Huh?" Ian laughed.

"Oh, you know what I mean."

He looked down at her, his blue eyes bright with amusement. "Yes, I guess I do know what you mean."

His fingers came to the side of her cheek and brushed back some stray locks of hair. The warmth of his touch was comforting against her skin.

"Let's get you home," he said.

"No, let's get *you* home," she countered, laughing.

"You're nearer."

"You're sicker."

"Okay then. Let's get me home."

He managed one good laugh before his coughing started again. She put her arm around his back and began leading him down the steps.

"I can still walk, you know."

"I know, but you're starting to shiver."

"You noticed that, huh?"

"Sure did." She pulled him in closer to her as they moved off into the chilly night.

12

Lori felt as though it was her first day at Lincoln High all over again. She glanced down the length of the lunchroom table and didn't know if she should attempt to join the girls already sitting there. She had been getting very cool responses throughout morning classes.

"Well, are you or aren't you?" Janis's voice demanded of her. "We only have thirty minutes in which to eat this so-called food."

Lori placed her tray at the end of the table and avoided looking at the other girls. Janis sat across from her and began lunch by eating her dessert first.

"Not that bad," she said, wiping her lips. "I can't figure out what flavor it's supposed to be, but at least it's smooth and creamy." She began poking at her entree with the spoon she had just used. "So, you getting all excited about tonight?" she asked.

"Tonight?"

"The dance, dummy. Do you think you could talk Ian into wearing a tuxedo too?"

"He's sick."

"Oh, I forgot." A look of concern spread across Janis's face. "Does this mean that you won't be . . . ?"

"Guess not," Lori said, inspecting her own tray.

"Oh, Lori, you have to come. You just have to. There are lots of guys who'd love to ask you, even if it's at the last minute."

"I think there are probably lots of guys at Lincoln High who'd be perfectly happy if I stayed at home."

"But not now, not since we found out you weren't what we thought you were, and you won't be messing in our lives anymore. Let me just think. Who could we get to take you? There's always my cousin Harold, but we only need to consider him if we get really desperate. Maybe if I asked John, he could come up with a list of possibilities, and we could go over them in Algebra and . . ."

"Janis, I really don't feel like going to the dance with just anybody."

"You mean it's Ian or nobody?"

"Yes," Lori said.

"Well, maybe he'll be better by tonight."

"Even if that's true, technically speaking he hasn't really asked me."

Janis's spoon clattered onto her plate. She stared at Lori in disbelief, too stunned to speak.

"You heard me," Lori said and laughed.

"But . . . but . . ." Janis sputtered.

"Now you really know what a non-expert I am when it comes to girl-boy relationships."

"But . . ."

"So it looks like you can tell me all about it in the morning," Lori said, digging into her noodles. She glanced down the table once again. "I wonder if I'm not the only one spending the evening at home?"

"Things will work out," Janis said. "Just as you always told us they would. But . . . oh, Lori, you can't stay at home tonight. I want you to be there in case I need moral support when John's tuxedo starts getting catcalls."

"Sorry, but you'll just have to deal with that alone, I'm afraid."

Janis pushed her entree aside and drew her salad to the front of her tray. "Maybe not," she said. "Maybe things will work out and Ian will ask you. He will if he uses his common sense."

Lori found that her own words, parroted back to her, held little comfort.

"Lori?" The girl was smiling at her hesitantly. She seemed wary about approaching too closely. "Are you in a hurry?" she asked.

Lori had only a few minutes to make her way all the way to the other end of the building for her next class, but she was so startled that the girl wanted to talk to her that she had stopped dead in her tracks.

"I just wanted to apologize for my outburst last night," the girl said, drawing closer. "Actually, I spoke too soon." She smiled nervously. "As you can see, I'm not in New York looking for an apartment. In fact, when I went home last night, my mother hadn't packed my bags at all. And she's letting me go to the dance tonight. Things have actually worked out okay."

"My advice was pretty terrible, though," said Lori.

"Well, I just wanted you to know that it really didn't ruin my life the way I thought it had last night. And it forced me to talk honestly with my mother about lots of things that . . . well, I'm sure you understand. Listen, I'm going to be late for chem lab, but I just wanted you to know that I'm not upset anymore. I'll be seeing you around, okay?"

A voice sounded loudly down the hallway as Lori approached.

"Of course he *is* a jerk, but he's the jerk I love, and I got so mad at him that I finally blurted it out this morning, and now . . . it's just the best it's ever been with us, and tonight is going to be incredible. Hey! Is that you, Lori Kennedy? Come over here. I have some amazing news to tell you. You wouldn't believe what's happened between . . ."

"I never realized how much fun a thirteen-year-old could be," the girl said, leaning against Lori's locker so that she couldn't get to her books. "It'll be a blast going with him! Who cares if I'm two years older? I know it's probably going to cause a scandal, but he's a really sharp dancer and knows all kinds of steps. Besides, it's kind of cute the way he looks up to me. . . ."

Lori tapped the bottom of the basket and the last of the leaves fell onto the pile next to the door.

"I told you they wouldn't stay mad at you for long," Janis said.

Lori stood back and surveyed the entranceway. "I'm a complete failure," she sighed.

"But it looks fantastic!"

"That's not what I'm talking about. No one listened at all to what I was saying last night. They're all starting to come up and thank me for that dumb advice I handed out yesterday and I can just sense that they want me to fall back into the same role all over again."

"So just tell them you won't."

"That's what I intend to do."

"Then what's your problem?"

"Oh, no," Lori said, spying a girl coming in the front door. "She looks as if she thinks she needs my advice desperately."

"Stop worrying."

The girl smiled as she drew nearer. "Hi, Lori," she said. "I just want you to know that I used my common sense and I said exactly what I thought I should say, and the results were very interesting. I mean *very interesting.*" Her giggle traveled along with her as she continued on to the gym.

"What was that all about?" Lori asked.

"You heard her. That one decided to use her

common sense and the results were *very interesting.*" Janis tried, but failed, to approximate the girl's giggle. "She won't be bothering you anymore."

"I hope not," Lori murmured, turning her attention back to the leaves.

The front door was pulled open again and a tall girl with oversized glasses came running toward them. "It works! It works!" she squealed. "I didn't beat around the bush at all, and everything I sensed about his feelings toward me is true! Oh, wow! Thanks Lori!"

"You see," Janis said as the girl pushed into the gym to tell her good news to other friends. "Some of them *were* listening."

"You really think so?"

"Of course. Look, Lori, some people are always going to need advice from others and some are perfectly capable of finding the solutions to their problems in themselves. That's just the way things are."

Lori sank down onto the leaf-strewn floor. "I just hope the ones who have to have advice find somebody who really knows what she's talking about. As far as this novice is concerned, office hours are over!"

Janis glanced down at the far end of the hallway. "Did Mrs. Rinehart say when we can dump the rest of the leaves along the sides?" she asked. "Do we have to wait till just before the dance begins, or can we do it now, so that we can get away from here early enough to get the leaf dirt out from under our nails?" Janis lifted her hands toward the overhead light. "It's going to take hours to deal with mine," she said with a loud laugh.

"She wants us to wait until later."

"Well, what are we supposed to do then? Wear heavy work gloves with our outfits?"

Lori struggled to her feet. "Don't worry," she said. "Tell the others they can all go now. I'll grab something to eat from the candy machine and stick around here. It won't matter how dirty my hands are."

"What makes you so sure you're not going to the dance?"

"Janis, just go and tell the others I'll see to the final batch of leaves. Stop feeling sorry for me and get on home. None of you is going to have that much time as it is."

Lori wandered slowly through the half-lit corridors of the building, stopping first at the pay phone near the school office to tell her mother that she'd be late getting home. By the time she finally reached the cafeteria, she wasn't sure that she felt like having a candy bar dinner. She inspected the apple machine. The fruit looked as green and sour as the one she had tried to eat last night. She opted for chocolate with nuts and nougat and a pint carton of milk. That would hold her until she got home.

She ate her snack at one of the tables and then made her way back to the gym. The hallway was deserted, but she could still hear sounds of last-minute preparations going on in the interior of the building. She began pulling the bushel baskets out from under the stairway where they had been stored. There was no reason why she couldn't begin to line the sides of the floor with high piles now that the hectic traffic of the decorating crews had ended.

The candy bar and the milk had given her an energy boost, and she was enjoying the physical activity of emptying the baskets. She took a certain satisfaction in watching the leaves flutter down and mount into banks of autumn colors. She could concentrate on that and not have to think about Ian home sick and herself about to depart for an evening in front of the television set with her family.

She pushed aside some stray leaves with her foot and inspected her efforts so far. It was going to be smashing, and she felt a glow of pride welling up inside her.

"Looks great," a raspy voice said from behind her.

She jumped slightly, not having heard the door open.

"Sorry. Didn't mean to scare you."

She turned slowly to face Ian. "You're not supposed to be here," she said. She was trying hard not to reveal the delight she was feeling at his presence in the hallway.

"I didn't exactly get up from my deathbed," he said.

"But I can tell you're not any better."

"I'll get there one of these days."

"Not if you keep running back out into the cold."

"It's not cold in here. Besides, I just figured out something this afternoon."

"And what was that?"

"What the missing element is."

"Missing element?"

"To make all of this perfect."

She looked down toward the door leading into the gym. "It's perfect enough."

"No, it's not," he said, suppressing a cough.

"Ian, go home and go back to bed."

"You see, what we need is more contrast."

"Ian . . ."

"Come on, now, listen. This is the artist in me speaking. I thought you were the one who wanted to encourage the reemergence of that fellow."

"He's already reemerged. This place is dazzling."

"But not perfect." He rubbed his hands through his mass of curly hair and then spread his arms wide. "What we need here is a touch of contrast. Are you willing to help me out?"

"Help you out how?"

"Get your jacket."

"Where are we going?"

"Just hush up and get your jacket."

"Ian . . ."

"We don't have much time."

"Are you crazy?"

His eyes looked into hers. "No, I think I'm just

coming to my senses," he murmured as he tugged her toward the door.

"Look, if *I'm* freezing, then you must be double-freezing. Let's turn back before we both catch pneumonia."

"You're acting as if it's the dead of winter," he teased.

"When the sun finally sets, it's going to *feel* like the dead of winter."

"We've still got a half hour before the sun disappears. That'll give us just enough time." Suddenly he came to a complete stop. "Oh, no," he said angrily. "We forgot to bring something to—Where's the nearest grocery store?"

"Grocery store?"

"Yeah, isn't there some little place right around here?"

"We already passed it."

"How far back?"

"Two blocks."

"Just stay where you are. I'll be back in a jiffy."

"What did you buy?"

He clutched the paper bag to his side. "Nothing exciting," he said. "Functional though."

"I see."

"You think we could start walking a little faster?"

"I thought you'd never ask."

"You're kidding!" she said, as they approached the familiar stone wall.

"It's the only place I'm sure we can find them."

"Ian, I'm not climbing over that thing again."

"Sure you are. We both are." He held the bag in one hand and quickly tossed it up in an arc so that it landed on the other side of the wall. "We have to now, don't we?" he laughed.

"Ian . . ."

"Come on, I'll give you a hand up."

"This is really crazy."

"No, it's not. Just catch on to the top rock and hoist yourself up."

"We're going to have the same trouble we did last time."

"You mean when I fell?"

"Yes, I mean when you fell."

"Oh, we've both been falling for awhile. We might as well accept the fact and enjoy it. Falling out of lofts, falling off walls, falling out of trees, falling into love."

Her hand seemed to freeze on the top rock.

"Hoist yourself up," he yelled. "I'll join you in a second."

Maybe she hadn't heard him right. Had she gone crazy too?

"Now that wasn't so difficult, was it?" he asked, once he was sitting beside her. "And there's our treasure down below."

"They're just leaves, Ian. You dragged us out here just to get more leaves?"

"Look closely, Lori. Those aren't just leaves. Those are *red* leaves. Wonderful, bold, ruby-colored, magnificent *red* leaves. Think of the contrast with all the yellows."

"Ian, you *have* gone crazy."

"I always was a perfectionist," he croaked. "Now come on. Let's get down there and start gathering up all those gorgeous things. On the count of three, let's both jump."

Miraculously, they both landed on their feet.

"Here. I've got a present for you," he said, reaching for the brown paper bag.

"A present?"

"Just calm down. It's definitely going to underwhelm you, but it *is* functional."

She could hear perforated cardboard ripping and then he swung around with a half-folded green plastic bag in his hand. "Now go to it," he said. "That sun isn't going to be much help in a few minutes, and I want to make sure we get only red ones."

"Red leaves, no matter how beautiful, aren't worth pneumonia," she said. Nevertheless, she leaned down and started to stuff her bag.

"But I want our first dance at Lincoln High to be memorable."

"Even though we're not going?"

He jammed a handful of leaves deep into the bag. "We're not?" he asked.

"You've got a bad cold," she reminded him.

"You're not allowed in with a cold?"

"Ian . . ."

"It's the sneakers, isn't it?" he said. "You don't want to be seen with a guy wearing sneakers. Look, we can't all be snappy dressers like John Kane."

"Ian . . ." Lori repeated.

He looked over at her. "What's wrong?" he asked.

"Are we about to ruin everything by having a fight?" she said, drawing a pile of leaves to her side.

"I don't want to fight with you. It's just that every once in awhile you get this look on your face as if you think I'm some kind of little kid. And I'm not, Lori. You think all of this is silly, but it's not. I really believe it's important to make that hallway look perfect."

She didn't know what to say. Her hand went to the leaves and stopped.

"Hey, look at me," he said softly. "Don't you realize how crazy I am about you? Your old pal at camp was always crazy about you too, but this is something different. It's true I didn't have any patience with that role you were playing for the others, but it wasn't that I was trying to keep you as just my buddy. I wanted the real grown-up you, and all that falseness kept getting in the way and then I started feeling scared that it was always going to get in the way and . . . well, I sure did mess things up for a while, didn't I?" He stifled a cough. "You didn't really believe there was some college girl, did you?"

She smiled. "No, not really."

"I didn't think you did. I don't know why a dumb thing like that popped from my mouth." He looked at her closely. "What are you thinking?" he asked finally. "What do you think about all I've just said?"

"I'm thinking that I . . . that I don't know what

you mean by the real grown-up me," she said shakily.

"I'm not sure if I can describe it," Ian said, moving closer. "It's just something I feel is there behind your eyes, something that's probably just as half-formed as it is in me, but I know it's there. Every so often I catch a glimpse of you and I think, 'That's a woman I'm looking at.'" He laughed. "Does any of this make sense?"

She nodded.

"Of course, I'm glad that I also can still catch glimpses of the girl you were back in camp. You see, that's why I think we have a real chance of working things out. We understand where we're coming from, and so many people have to spend ages figuring that out. Or does that make us boring to each other?"

"You're far from boring," Lori said solemnly.

"Ditto," he said, as solemn as Lori was. His face moved slowly toward hers. "I don't want to risk giving you my cold," he murmured. "So this will have to do until I'm better. Consider it a rain-check." His lips brushed gently against her fore-head and he drew back.

"Wait," she whispered. She laced her fingers into the hair at the back of his neck and drew him closer. "This is to get better on," she said, as she shyly kissed his lips.

"I never realized leaves were this heavy," Lori said as she struggled up the steps of the gym with the two plastic bags. "Thank goodness we had a car when we got the other ones."

"Stop complaining. It will be worth the effort."

Lori paused at the top step and looked at her watch. She listened to the sound of the music coming from inside the building. "Are you sure this is going to be worth it? The dance has been on for over an hour now. Everyone's here who's going to be here. They've already seen the entranceway."

"They have to leave that way, don't they?" Ian said. "We'll give them something to remember when they go home."

"Wait a minute! There's somebody pulling up to the curb right now. Quick, let's rush inside and scatter the leaves!"

"How come you're so enthusiastic all of a sudden?" Ian laughed.

"Come on!" Lori said, pulling open the door and trying to lift the bags at the same time.

Once inside, they had trouble undoing the twist-ties. Ian had just begun to place handfuls of the leaves near the entrance to the gym when the outside door began to open.

"Wait a minute!" Lori yelled out. "Don't come in yet!"

"What does she mean, don't come in yet!" Janis's loud voice said indignantly. "We're already over an hour late because you-know-who's nifty outfit didn't arrive on time, and now she wants us to wait outside? What's going on in there?"

"Just wait a few more seconds."

The door began pushing open anyway.

"Janis!"

"How come you're still here?" her friend asked,

peering down the hallway. She spotted Ian. "Oh," she said, her face breaking into a smile. "I see you *are* going to the dance after all." Her eyes took in Lori's clothes. "Well, sort of," she said. "So why can't we come in?"

"Ian's adding the missing element."

"More leaves?"

"Red ones. Wait 'til you see how they contrast with the yellows."

Janis pushed all the way into the hall. "Yes, it's a nice touch," she said with a distracted air. "I guess maybe it's better we did arrive late. That way no one will notice us sneaking into the gym, and then maybe we can hide behind one of those haystacks."

"Where's John?"

"Good question," Janis said. "He was right behind me." She pushed open the door and peered out. "What's holding you up?" she said crossly.

"I had to redo the tie," John's voice said from the steps. "It was coming undone."

"Well, get in here. It's only Lori and Ian. They won't laugh too much."

John entered the hallway slowly.

Lori's eyes widened in surprise. "But it looks great!" she said.

"It does?" Janis squinted at her date. "What do you think, Ian?"

Ian moved toward them from the far end of the hallway. "I don't know, Janis," he said. "Maybe you'd better march him out of here right now."

"Ridiculous, right?"

"When those other girls get a look at him all

spiffed up like this, you'd better hold on tight if you want someone to take you home."

"You mean he looks okay?"

"He's . . . resplendent."

"Resplendent?"

"A knockout," Lori added.

"Really? You know, I sort of thought that too, but I didn't want to say anything in front of him in case he got . . . a knockout, huh?"

"I told you it would look nifty," John said, winking at Lori.

"You got the tickets?" Janis asked.

John patted the side of his jacket and nodded.

"Well, let's get in there then and show Lincoln High what nifty is."

Lori and Ian watched with amusement as the couple made their way along the hall, Janis talking a mile a minute the whole time.

"I don't think perfection made much of an impact on them," Ian said as the two disappeared into the gym.

"Are you finished?"

"Finished! We've got three more bags to work with."

"Well, then, let's go to work. Your cold is sounding worse by the minute."

"I'm surviving," he said, giving in to a cough.

They moved as quickly as possible up and down the hall, adding the leaves to the piles and stepping back from time to time to view the effect. Ian made some adjustments to the lighting so that the walls began to take on an autumn glow. By the time they were finished they knew that the students attending the dance were going to exit into something spectacular that evening.

Ian stuffed the plastic bags under the stairwell and he and Lori stood at the far end of the hallway surveying their final efforts.

"Not quite perfection," Ian said hoarsely.

"It is too!"

"There's still something missing from the evening."

"What?"

"My first dance at Lincoln High."

"Ian, you're in no shape to go inside there. Neither of us is dressed for it, and I'll bet you don't even have tickets. You need to get home and—"

"Hey, I didn't say I wanted to go inside. All I said was that there was something missing, namely, my first dance at Lincoln High."

"What do you mean?"

"I mean this," he said, pulling her to his side and starting to sway to the sound of the music coming from the gym. "Just one dance and then I'll let you take me home." His arms encircled her and they began moving down the hall between the piles of leaves. She rested her head against his chest and gave herself up to the warmth that enclosed her.

"Lori?"

"What?"

"It *is* kind of magical, isn't it? I mean, tonight could have been terrible for both of us, and now . . ."

"The song's ending. Let's get out of here."

"You really want to leave?"

"You should go home," she murmured.

"Is that your advice?" He grinned.

"Yes."

"Okay, pal. Let's get out of here." They pulled apart, but he didn't let go of her hand. "But let's take it kind of slow," he said. "Let's take it in time to the music."

Genuine Silhouette sterling silver bookmark for only $15.95!

What a beautiful way to hold your place in your current romance! This genuine sterling silver bookmark, with the distinctive Silhouette symbol in elegant black, measures 1½" long and 1" wide. It makes a beautiful gift for yourself, and for every romantic you know! And, at only $15.95 each, including all postage and handling charges, you'll want to order several now, while supplies last.

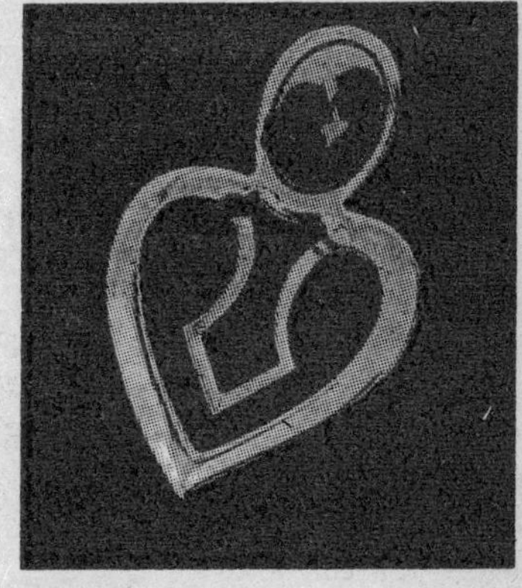

Send your name and address with check or money order for $15.95 per bookmark ordered to
Simon & Schuster Enterprises
120 Brighton Rd., P.O. Box 5020
Clifton, N.J. 07012
Attn: Bookmark

Bookmarks can be ordered pre-paid only. No charges will be accepted. Please allow 4-6 weeks for delivery.

N.Y. State Residents
Please Add Sales Tax

53 ☐ LIGHT OF MY LIFE Harper
54 ☐ PICTURE PERFECT Enfield
55 ☐ LOVE ON THE RUN Graham
56 ☐ ROMANCE IN STORE Arthur
57 ☐ SOME DAY MY PRINCE Ladd
58 ☐ DOUBLE EXPOSURE Hawkins
59 ☐ A RAINBOW FOR ALISON Johnson
60 ☐ ALABAMA MOON Cole
61 ☐ HERE COMES KARY! Dunne
62 ☐ SECRET ADMIRER Enfield
63 ☐ A NEW BEGINNING Ryan
64 ☐ MIX AND MATCH Madison
65 ☐ THE MYSTERY KISS Harper
66 ☐ UP TO DATE Sommers
67 ☐ PUPPY LOVE Harrell
68 ☐ CHANGE PARTNERS Wagner
69 ☐ ADVICE AND CONSENT Alexander
70 ☐ MORE THAN FRIENDS Stuart
71 ☐ THAT CERTAIN BOY Malek
72 ☐ LOVE AND HONORS Ryan

Tired of the winter blahs?
Enjoy an
ENDLESS SUMMER
by Rose Bayner Coming in January.

FIRST LOVE, Department FL/4
1230 Avenue of the Americas
New York, NY 10020

Please send me the books I have checked above. I am enclosing $___________ (please add 75¢ to cover postage and handling. NYS and NYC residents please add appropriate sales tax). Send check or money order—no cash or C.O.D.'s please. Allow six weeks for delivery.

NAME ____

ADDRESS ____

CITY _________________________________ STATE/ZIP _________________

Coming Next Month

A Passing Game by Beverly Sommers

As kicker and only girl on the Evanston High football team, Tobey basked in glory. And to top it all, she was on a personal kick of her own: should she run for the touchdown, block or intercept an unexpected pass?

Under The Mistletoe by Michelle Mathews

Her father was shocked, her mother astounded when a handsome stranger took Megan in his arms and tenderly kissed her under the mistletoe. But as for Megan—she rather enjoyed it. It was definitely going to be one of the better Christmas vacations.

Send In The Clowns by Marilyn Youngblood

Lita's heart was doing somersaults. She couldn't stop grinning. Her life was a circus! Now that she had met Jerry, she was dancing on a tightrope. But would he hold the net? Did he really plan to include her in his act?

Short Stop For Romance by Elaine Harper

Celia nearly flipped when she found out that her mother had hired Mark Maxwell to dog-sit while the Clinton family went off to a family reunion. Why he was just about the most attractive guy in Blossom Valley High! Now she would have a chance to get to know him.

READERS' COMMENTS ON FIRST LOVE BOOKS

"I am very pleased with the First Love Books by Silhouette. Thank you for making a book that I can enjoy."

—G.O.*, Indianapolis, IN

"I just want you to know that I love the Silhouette First Love Books. They put me in a happy mood. Please don't stop selling them!"

—M.H.*, Victorville, CA

"I loved the First Love book that I read. It was great! I loved every single page of it. I plan to read many more of them."

—R.B.*, Picayune, MS

* names available upon request